Shangri-La
By
Christopher Cartwright

Prologue

Somewhere over the Bay of Bengal, India – 1931

The starlit sky turned ominous, as dark and angry clouds descended.

The pilot tried to fly beneath the clouds, but the darkness continued to envelop the aircraft like an impenetrable cloak. In the inky black sky, a bolt of lightning streaked, lighting up the outside world for an instant, while simultaneously filling the inside with the violent crack of thunder.

The Avro 652, a twin engine, low-wing monoplane with a retractable carriage, and tailwheel bounced around with the storm, its delicate fuselage being blown about like a dragonfly in the wind. The aircraft had left Colombo, Sri Lanka, two hours earlier as part of its nightly Karachi-Bombay-Colombo mail service.

James Hilton roused with a jolt, his heart pounding in his chest. His eyes opened wide, his pupils large like saucers, scanned out the port window expecting to see fire. Instead, he saw nothing but darkness staring back at him. He turned his head to starboard to see if everything was okay and was greeted by more darkness.

He swallowed down the fear and panic that had risen, his eyes searching the aircraft for any sign of disaster. He sighed, trying to get comfortable again. He'd been sleeping midway along the heavily overloaded cargo hold, in a makeshift seat between a series of canvas mail bags and the starboard bulkhead of the fuselage.

Hilton planted his hands behind his head, shuffled backward, and forced himself to close his eyes. Even a little bit of sleep before he reached Karachi would make a difference to his day tomorrow, he told himself.

He began counting to ten, reassuring himself that if the little aircraft flew safely for ten seconds there was no reason it wouldn't keep on doing so. It was a silly game, but after several of these rough flights in remote areas, he'd learned that it helped his mind settle.

Hilton only reached eight.

The Avro 652 hit a pocket of air, dropping suddenly in the turbulence with a loud clank that sounded like it had ripped the wings right off the airframe. James sat bolt upright. He could feel the blood pulsating in the back of his neck. This time he knew he was up for the rest of the flight.

His intelligent, deep-set eyes stared out into the pitch darkness beyond the narrow window. His eyes fixed on the void. It was impossible to see anything. They were probably thousands of feet off the ground, anyway.

A nearby lightning flash, followed by a near instantaneous boom of thunder, revealed the white caps of a turbulent sea not so far below. The aircraft shuddered, as though it, too, were concerned by the incoming lightning storm. He bit his lower lip and consciously took a deep breath. The pilot had presumably taken them down low in an attempt to avoid the worst of the turbulence. James wasn't so sure it had made a difference, everything still seemed shaky as hell.

A series of violent explosions, progressively getting closer.

From the cockpit, the pilot shouted, "You'd better hang on back there… this is about to get a little bumpy."

James gripped a steel strut for support, feeling his back suddenly dig into the mail bag he was using as a seat.

James asked, "Are we going to be okay?"

"Sure," the pilot replied, his voice relaxed and congenial. "Nothing particularly unusual. Just a bit of rough weather. There's a storm I'm trying my best to overcome. I've seen worse."

James wasn't sure if he took the pilot's insouciance as comforting or disconcerting. Either way, there was nothing he could do about it now. He felt the Avro 652 shift and sway, as its pilot banked and attempted to dart the small aircraft out of the storm. The nose tilted upward, and the twin Armstrong Siddeley Cheetah VI seven-cylinder air-cooled radial engine whined under the new pressure, as the pilot attempted to extract every last one of the 290 horses out of the engines. They sounded strained.

A freelance journalist by trade, James Hilton began to doubt his decision to enlist the help of the nightly mail service to speed up his transport to Karachi, Pakistan, to write his article. The airfare had been cheap, but the aircraft and cowboy-like pilot were becoming dubious.

More lightning flashed and the pilot increased power to the engines to stave off stalling as he climbed at what felt like a near vertical rate.

A loud explosion erupted from the starboard engine. It sounded like shards of metal grinding on metal, followed by the engine straining to overcome an unseen obstacle. James glued his eyes on the outside wingtip, where the engine whined at a feverish pitch. It was all dark, making it impossible to see the engine, but he could hear it. Hilton wasn't a mechanic, but what he heard didn't sound good. Another bolt of lightning filled the sky, revealing the outline of the damaged engine.

He took in a breath, and cursed.

In the darkness, the engine cowling ripped open, erupting in flame. The blaze trailed from the engine, extending several feet behind the wing. The Avro 652 hung in there for a few seconds more before the magic seemed to disappear. The starboard wing dipped first, before the pilot – correcting for the stall – lowered the nose sharply, exchanging his hard-earned altitude for airspeed.

James, now fully roused from his stupor, clambered across the cargo through his makeshift sleeping arrangements, toward the cockpit. He slipped past the pilot, into the copilot seat and strapped himself in. There was a certain finality to the way the seatbelt made a metallic clicking sound as it locked together.

He turned to the pilot who was actively working the seemingly endless myriad of controls to regain the unyielding will of the falling aircraft. His mouth agape, he stared at the pilot, who either didn't notice him or was too busy trying to save their lives to care.

James collected himself and said, "The engine… do you know it's on fire?"

The pilot appeared undaunted. "Yeah… I kind of noticed."

James waited for the pilot to inform him of their next course of action, but the man didn't seem to be forthcoming with one.

In his head, he counted to five. "Should we do something about the fire?"

The pilot shrugged. "Sure, there's a fire extinguisher behind your seat. Why don't you go back there and put it out for me?"

"Fire extinguisher… right… good idea." James ran his eyes across the fire extinguisher, through to the flaming engine on the starboard side. There was no way in the world he could reach the flame while they were in the air. "How do I reach it? Do I need to climb out on the wing or something?"

The pilot grinned. "Yeah, that would be great."

James swallowed hard, and rising to the occasion, he went to unclip his seatbelt.

The pilot put a hand on the belt. "I was kidding, you fool!"

James glanced at the pilot. The man looked confident, almost bored by their near-death experience. He wasn't sure if this meant he should feel reassured by this or concerned at the state of the pilot's grasp on reality. Either way, his entire world was spinning. He nodded vacantly, lost in the surreal events unfolding. "Oh, right."

He stared out at the darkness through the cockpit windshield. Rain pummeled the windshield and he wondered how the pilot could see anything.

Suddenly, the darkness gave way to the light of a ship. Some sort of cargo vessel by the looks of things. James expelled a breath, feeling relieved. Somehow the sight of the ship meant they were no longer alone in the middle of an endless ocean. They were close enough he could make out the name of the ship along its portside.

Shinyō Maru

The Avro 652 looked like it was going to run straight into it.

The pilot banked to starboard. His face reflecting fear for the first time. "Oh shit!"

James stared at the ship. There was a boy on the deck. The kid seemed to be no more than five or six and seemed so out of place that for a split second, his mind was distracted from his imminent death. He blinked.

And the pilot pulled the Avro 652 around the ship's bow.

The aircraft leveled out just above the sea, before the pilot managed to increase enough thrust to the port propeller, so that they could climb again.

Up ahead, the seemingly endless sea gave way to a jagged coastline and mountains that stretched up to the gods.

The Avro 652 climbed slowly.

James, realizing the pilot intended to climb the mountains, said, "What are you doing? You'll never cross it! Shouldn't we go back to Colombo?"

The pilot shook his head. "No. It's too far. When the starboard engine exploded, it must have taken out part of the fuel feeding line, so we won't have enough to get back there. Our only hope is to climb the range and hope to find somewhere to land."

"We're losing fuel?"

"Afraid so."

"How much?"

"All of it."

"How long do we have?"

"I don't know. Probably about half an hour. Maybe longer."

James tried to do arithmetic in his head, making sense of the geometry. The only mountains in the region were massive. There was no way they could overcome any of them with that little fuel and there was nowhere to land.

Which meant, they were flying to their deaths.

The pilot nursed the port engine urging it to keep going and the Avro 652 continued to climb. The altimeter kept turning in a clockwise direction and the air continued to become thinner. James watched in silence.

They were both praying for a miracle.

Below them, the snow-covered ground revealed nothing but vertical drops, valleys, and rocky passes miles high, but nowhere to put the aircraft down – certainly not in one piece.

James, unable to keep it to himself, finally said, "We're not going to make it are we?"

The pilot shook his head. "Not a chance in hell."

"Right…" James said, unable to think of anything better to say.

They continued for another few minutes, before the portside engine stuttered, and choked to a stop, the propeller stood still. The pilot, prepared for the sudden loss in power, gently lowered the nose, dipping the aircraft to maintain airspeed and prevent the inevitable stall. They were out of fuel. With both engines stopped, the Avro 652 was destined to plummet to the Earth.

James searched the landscape below for somewhere to land. It seemed impossible to him that this should be it. That his otherwise uninspiring life should end like this. He still had infinite hopes and dreams.

He used his hands to brace against the front of the cockpit as though, through sheer strength of will, he could prevent it falling out of the sky.

Holding his breath, he watched as the altimeter spun in a counterclockwise direction.

The pilot, shifting the controls with confident and adept movements, trimmed the aircraft's downward trajectory so that it would reach the snow-covered pass between two mountain peaks – at the end of which, appeared a drop into oblivion thousands of feet below.

James glanced at his pilot. The man appeared calm, not disinterested, but hardly concerned. The image gave him hope. "Are we going to make it?"

The pilot shrugged. "Who can say?"

And with that, the Avro 652 fell from the sky.

The nose dipped and the cockpit raced downward like a rollercoaster plummeting to the ground below. Snow and ice whipped the windshield.

The pilot kept the landing gear retracted in an attempt to maintain airspeed and to allow the fuselage to act like a ski.

The Avro 652 struck the icy crest, skimming the surface of the first peak, before its momentum carried it across to the second peak part flight part crash, where it began to slide down the split between the pass.

Snow pummeled the windshield.

It ran across the small field of icy whiteness before coming to a sudden stop.

The nose struck stone buried beneath the snow. In an instant, the entire aluminum nose of the aircraft crumpled, and the aircraft came to a complete stop. James flew forward, his head striking the windshield...

Knocking him out cold.

*

James Hilton became aware of the throbbing pain in his head as consciousness slowly returned. His vision blurry... no, not just blurry. It was so dark he couldn't see anything. He closed his eyes and concentrated on his other senses. There was the sound of liquid leaking onto metal somewhere up behind him. His first thought was that the crash had severed the fuel lines, but then he remembered they'd run out of fuel, so it was unlikely to be enough to cause an explosion.

He felt a small trickle of warm blood run down his forehead. He wiped it with the sleeve of his jacket and then took stock of his injuries by running his hands over himself. He had a throbbing headache, a small laceration over his forehead that was far from being life threatening, and he'd knocked his left knee on something leaving a large swollen bump where his patella belonged. He tentatively extended his leg. It hurt, but it wasn't going to kill him and it wasn't broken as far as he could tell.

He took a deep breath and exhaled.

He was hurt, but given the sort of plane crash he'd just survived, he was in a pretty good condition.

James opened his eyes and surveyed his new surroundings. It was still dark. Everything was dark. He blinked and rubbed his eyes, fighting down the panic that was raising like the tide, and threatening to overcome him.

Had the injuries to his head made him blind?

James wiped the blood from his brow, hoping it would reveal the cause of his lost sight. It didn't. He couldn't see anything. Not even the haze of a distant outline. He felt his heart race. He was blind. Or else he was buried in darkness? Perhaps the crash had caused an avalanche, leaving him trapped deep beneath the snow in a shroud of infinite blackness befitting those who were permanently buried six feet below.

The thought didn't exactly fill him with relief. He suppressed the fear and searched through his pockets for something that would at least let him know which type of nightmare he'd found himself within.

He felt the seam of his right pocket, sifting through the garbled mess of assorted items that had previously been discarded there with no apparent reasoning before boarding the flight at the last minute. His passport and wallet, once so valuable, now seemed irrelevant to him. He plucked them out, made sure that he hadn't caught anything else in their hold, and returned to the now emptier pocket.

James huffed. "For God's sake, where did it go?"

The pocket was empty.

He frowned and shifted his search efforts to his left pocket. He had no more luck with that pocket than the right.

Fear kept rising in his throat despite his best efforts to quell it.

Then he felt something weighty shift in his front shirt pocket. James held his breath. He tentatively reached inside until his fingers gripped something cold and metal. His fingers withdrew the *Morlite* cigarette lighter.

He exhaled gently.

Gripping the metal casing in his right hand with the adept skills of a habitual smoker, he spun the flint roller with his thumb and a golden flame ignited, reassuring him that he wasn't blind, but instead, was now trapped beneath the remnants of an avalanche.

The thought didn't reassure him much, as he realized he might be trapped. It wasn't great, but it was better than being blind he decided, a little more confidently than before.

His gaze turned to the pilot. The man looked like he'd sustained more significant injuries and, if even alive, he hadn't woken up yet.

Hilton unclipped his restraint and checked on the man, placing a sympathetic hand on the pilot's shoulder. He said, "Are you okay, buddy?"

The man moaned, but didn't make much more of an audible response.

Hilton wished he'd bothered to get the man's name before they had taken off. He watched the man's chest rise and fall. The pilot was still breathing, but the breath was labored. Hilton's gaze drifted downward, where he spotted the source of the pilot's injuries.

A large shard of aluminum, ripped free from the nose of the aircraft had fractured and imbedded into the man's abdomen. There was blood everywhere. Even without any medical training, Hilton knew his only companion wouldn't survive.

He stood up, leaving the pilot to die in peace and headed aft, along the fuselage and cargo hold to assess how bad things really were.

The cargo had all shifted forward in the crash, taking him several minutes to clear the wreckage.

The second half of the fuselage had been ripped apart in the crash, leaving a gash in the aluminum skin roughly five feet apart.

Snow had filled the opening, but a casual assessment showed it to be soft and readily movable. Hilton, who was an avid mountaineer knew enough about avalanches and snow types to feel reasonably confident in his ability to tunnel a way out. Although where he'd go after that, he was much less optimistic.

His mind turned to his next priority. He would need supplies. He opened the first cargo bag. It was filled with mail. No food, water, or warm clothes. He opened the next one, followed by another, but with the exception of paper to burn, there were no materials of any use to him. The fourth one had a bag of rice. He stuffed the bag into his backpack, alongside the few things of value to him now. After the fifth, the flame on his *Morlite* began to flicker.

For a moment, he panicked that the flame would extinguish and he would be left in total darkness. He frantically searched the cockpit and found a flashlight next to a first aid kit. Hilton pulled out the first aid kit, stuffing it into his backpack and switched on the flashlight, saving what remained of his *Morlite* lighter for later when he would most likely need it to start a fire.

Next to the dead or at least dying pilot – he really wasn't quite sure which – Hilton spotted a hand drawn map of the region. It was rudimentary compared to a typical topographical map drawn up by a professional cartographer. Instead, this one appeared to be more like a series of key landscapes, most likely handmade by the pilot himself, as navigational references.

Hilton fixed his flashlight on the map. It showed the rough topographical outline from Sri Lanka in the south, through to China in the north, with the Bay of Bengal and the large mountain range of the Himalayas in the middle.

He sighed. *Great. No problem. I'm somewhere in the middle of nowhere.* That much he knew without thinking, but the question remained, where exactly within that desolate mountain range did the Avro 652 go down?

And more importantly, where the hell was he going to go?

Hilton folded the map and placed it in his left trouser pocket, before turning to leave the wreckage of the aircraft.

He took two steps and stopped.

Because the near-dead pilot was now awake. His arm, rising like some sort of fiendish ghoul, moved to grab Hilton's leg.

*

Hilton stared at the pilot in horror.

The man had sustained substantial injuries. The pilot had been unrousable a few minutes earlier, and Hilton was almost certain when he glanced at him while going through the map, that he had passed away.

Hilton stared at him in silence, uncertain what to say to the dying man. His eyes narrowed in on the man's face. Where it had been drained of all color a few minutes earlier, it was flushed and animated now.

The pilot broke the silence. "Are you hurt?"

"No." Hilton replied, almost feeling guilty. "It appears I fared better than you."

"Yes. I believe I'm going to die." The pilot nodded, speaking matter-of-factly. "The question is, will you survive?"

Hilton could hear the challenge in the man's voice. He drew a quick breath and retrieved the rudimentary map. "I suppose that all depends on where we landed."

The pilot looked distracted, his eyes gazed across the cockpit, as though searching for something he'd misplaced.

Hilton watched him for a moment. "Hey, what are you looking for?"

The pilot's eyes drifted toward a secret compartment. "Behind the copilot seat there's a small latch. If you turn it upward, a hidden drawer opens up. I need you to retrieve something for me."

Hilton nodded. "Right."

He felt behind the copilot's seat, his fingers feeling a small wooden latch. He pulled on it, and a small compartment opened in the flooring.

He peered inside, expecting to find something of value. Instead, there was a small metal medallion.

He withdrew it to examine it in the light.

The medallion was made out of some sort of bronze and brass alloy. Quite dull to look at and most likely worthless. He examined the face of the medallion. There was a single image. It had two circles that stood side by side to form the number 8 lying on its side, possibly forming a geometric figure called a lemniscate – or the mathematical sign for infinity.

On closer inspection, the two circles were more than just that. They depicted a snake biting its tail. There were eight barely visible markings spread out along equal points of the circle, making him wonder if the whole thing actually was just the number 8? He took another glance at the medallion as a whole and wondered if something about the image made him think of ancient Egypt.

He suppressed a grin. "What the hell is it?"

"Something entirely worthless, yet priceless."

Hilton's eyes drifted between the useless relic and the dying pilot. "What do you want me to do with it?"

"I need you to grant me a last request…"

"Hey buddy, in case you haven't realized there's still very little chance I'm getting off this mountain alive."

"Please, it's important. Can you deliver something for me?"

"Okay, okay." Hilton asked, "Where do you want me to take it?"

The pilot didn't answer.

He looked like he'd passed out again.

Hilton glanced at the blood now flowing freely from the wound in the man's lower abdomen. It wouldn't be long now. The man would surely die.

Frustrated, Hilton held out the map in front of the pilot. "I need you to concentrate… can you show me where to go?"

The pilot's eyes suddenly widened, as though he willed his body to remain alive just a few minutes more. He looked at the map. "Head north…"

Hilton glanced at the map. "North? There's nothing there... it's just more mountains... I'd never make it..."

"There's a lamasery. The monks there will protect you..."

"A lamasery?"

"A monastery of Buddhist lamas."

"Oh? Where?"

"The locals call it Shangri-La. Please, bring them the medallion."

Hilton grabbed the pilot and tried to rouse him. But the man's purple eyes rolled into the back of his head.

He checked for a pulse. There wasn't one, at least not one that he could feel.

Hilton glanced at the pilot wondering if there was perhaps something he should at least try and do. A large piece of steel looked like it had penetrated his abdomen. He grimaced. There was nothing that he could do to save the man, even if he was a doctor, or inclined to help, which he wasn't.

He turned and said, "I'm sorry."

He then clambered out of the gaping hole in the mangled wreckage of the aluminum fuselage.

The ground was deep with snow. He walked to the end of the ridge and looked out. As far as his eyes could see was a barren and unforgiving landscape, an inhospitable land of snow and ice. He pulled out the rudimentary map and glanced at it.

To the south was the Bay of Bengal. Even if he could reach it, there was no way to cross the ocean and find help. To the north, nothing but giant mountain peaks, that crested the horizon like the buttress of a fortress... impenetrable mountains. He was an avid mountaineer, but without any equipment he would never climb it.

His eyes narrowed, and the creases in his face deepened, as he considered the position he was in. Either direction would lead to his certain death. To the east and west there were no signs of civilization for hundreds of miles.

That left one option, albeit a crazy one.

He could head north, in search of the near mythical lamasery, hidden away from the civilizations of the world, high in the Himalayan mountains.

With that thought, he set the compass of his arrow north, and began his impossible journey to a place he wasn't even sure existed.

In search of Shangri-La.

*

Over the course of the next three days Hilton braved the sub-freezing conditions by constantly moving throughout the day, and taking shelter in half buried snow caves at night. There were no trails in the snow or signs of a concealed pathway. Nothing to suggest that any living humans ever traversed the snow-covered mountains.

He navigated by sight, judging as he walked which passes were capable of being climbed or traversed. On two occasions, he got the choice wrong, only to find out after several hours of walking that the route was impassable.

He melted ice to drink by placing it in a tin bowl and setting it in the sun, and chewed on uncooked rice for nutrients. It wasn't a lot, barely enough to sustain the high caloric expenditure of mountaineering.

As the days went on, what little weight he once carried, was stripped from his body, taking with it all energy. He was a determined man, driven onward by survival instincts and his will to live.

But as days turned into weeks, his mind, and eventually his will to survive was drawn from his body until he was stripped bare.

In the distance, he kept his eyes fixed on the largest mountain peak. Each day, he strived to reach it. That was his giant. His goal. An insurmountable barricade. He kept going, spurring himself on with his single objective – to cross that mountain.

As his energy waned, he struggled to walk. The air thinned, and his breathing became labored even at rest. His vision blurred and he began to hallucinate. At first, he fought the hallucinations, as though he could defeat them, as he would any other obstacle that needed to be overcome. But as time went on, they became too difficult to fight.

Soon the intermittent hallucinations became an almost constant to him. He no longer had to walk the arduous journey alone. Instead, old friends walked with him to keep him company. A lover from his youthful days at Cambridge. A friend who died in an automobile accident in Brighton in the early 1920s.

It wasn't long before it was no longer the hallucinations he tried to fight off, but instead, it was reality that he resented. Soon after that he finally succumbed, and was no longer able to tell between the hallucinations and reality.

And still, he kept walking.

One foot in front of the other, until he reached the top. Taking one step at a time, he finally achieved his goal. He stepped up to the crest, and looked down upon a deep valley, above which, an even larger mountain shadowed it.

The sight crushed his soul.

For him, everything was over. He'd long since run out of food and no amount of optimism could encourage him to believe that he had enough energy in reserve to survive the days of strenuous hiking to reach the crest of the next mountain.

No, it was over for him.

With that thought, having lost the will to fight anything anymore, he took a step and stumbled, falling down the steep northern slope.

He didn't bother to try and arrest his descent. He didn't have the strength, and even if he did, he didn't have the will.

Better that he should fall to his death.

Hilton's speed picked up, as his downward progression reached a speed that would inevitably lead to his death. He tumbled, round and round, like a ragdoll as he fell down the snow-covered slope. His body hit a small mound in the snow at thirty miles an hour, sending him flying into the air.

He waited to land, but the landing didn't seem to come.

Instead, he just kept falling.

He tried to open his eyes, but his vision was failing him. He was now certain he'd gone off one of the vertical ledges that descended thousands upon thousands of feet.

It was like that dream that everyone's had at one stage or another. You know the one where you're falling and if you ever hit the ground you're certain you will die, only, instead of dying, you simply wake up. Only, in this case, Hilton knew he was travelling at such a speed that he would never wake up.

Curiously, his mind wondered if he would even register hitting the ground. Of course, it wouldn't. The whole thing would happen so fast that his brain wouldn't have time to register it. Even so, he struggled to imagine being alive one minute, and dead the next.

A few seconds later, his body struck something hard and smooth. He kept falling. Only he was no longer free falling. His body was sliding down a near vertical shaft. Something so steep that he could barely feel his body press up against the back of it.

For a moment, he thought he'd just survived a miracle.

And then his head struck something hard, and he was knocked out cold.

James Hilton's consciousness returned slowly in ebbs and flows.

His hearing was the first to return. He could hear the sound of people – a couple women and possibly a man – splashing in nearby water. The frontal cortex, the aspect of his brain dedicated to reasoning and logic wasn't firing much at all yet, but he knew something about the information coming in didn't quite match the data already there.

Why would anyone be splashing in water in the freezing Himalayan mountains?

He tried to open his eyes but only darkness entered. Time passed and soon a series of sensations swept his body. He could feel the warm touch of sun as it gently kissed his skin, and the mild almost equatorial sea breeze tease his face.

The slightest of grins creased James Hilton's chapped lips.

Well I'll be damned... there is an afterlife.

As consciousness fully returned, he opened his eyes, and slowly eased himself up onto his feet. There was another bump on the back of his head, showing where he'd fallen, but whatever had happened, he certainly didn't belong wherever he was now.

He patted himself down, trying to determine if he was dead or alive. He glanced back at the small cave in which he'd come out of. He stared inside. The thing was dark made from some sort of perfectly smooth stone that seemed to reflect every shimmer of light as adequately as a mirror as it formed a tunnel that seemed to extend forever.

Hilton stepped out of the cave and spotted a second cave next to it. He leaned in, hoping to see something that made sense, but pulled himself back with a jolt. His heart raced. The ground of the cave appeared to fall away like an endless abyss.

There was strange writing on the wall, in an equally unique script, he'd never seen before. There was no way to tell what it could possibly mean.

But below it, was an emblem that he recognized.

It depicted two circles that stood side by side to form the number 8 lying on its side. Each circle showed a snake biting its tail. The identical image as the one he'd seen on the medallion the pilot had given him.

Still unsure about what it meant, his eyes turned upward toward the giant vertical wall of hanging gardens, unlike anything he'd ever seen. They seemed like something out of the biblical Garden of Eden, with an array of tropical plants growing out of a giant vertical wall that stretched hundreds of feet high in every direction, hanging miraculously from the sky like a giant, tropical shroud.

Hilton squinted against the bright sky through which a warm sunlight poured down upon him. There was something unusual about the beam of sunlight. His eyes narrowed and he tried to work out what it was, but he couldn't put his finger on it. If he had to guess, it just seemed like something was slightly off. As though the light was being dispersed by something opaque.

His eyes drifted to the left, as he slowly turned around, taking in the entire enclave. At the center of which, was a small, almost medieval hamlet consisting of no more than a dozen or so stone houses, interspaced with a single large building at the center.

At the center of which, was a large, natural oasis with crystal clear water, surrounded by sand that looked entirely out of place high in the Himalayan mountains. A woman and her two small children played at the edge of the water.

On a deck of cedar, overlooking the oasis, a man in a Hawaiian shirt appeared to be tending what looked like some sort of bar – although if it was, it was the first time he'd heard of a lamasery in which the monks were able to drink alcohol. In fact, looking at it now, Hilton figured the refuge looked more like a luxurious tropical resort than a religious place of isolation.

The entire place smelled of the strong scents of exotic fruits which grew freely along the hanging gardens. Starving, he plucked a pitaya and a mangosteen. He pocketed the pitaya and ripped open the hard, leathery shell of the mangosteen, devouring it in a matter of seconds.

He tried to step toward the bar, but his legs gave out on him, and he stumbled onto the ground. Someone from the bar noticed, and rushed to his aid.

Supporting him from his shoulders, the man helped him to a seat at the bar. The man ran his eyes across him with a mixture of concern and respect. "I see you've made quite the journey to reach us?"

Hilton nodded, a suppressed grin on his lips, his eyes wandering across what he could only imagine were the surreal grounds of the utopian lamasery that the pilot had spoken off, named, Shangri-La. "Yeah, you can say that again."

"It's okay," the man reassured him, pouring him a beer from the tap without asking if he wanted one. "That's normal. Not many people survive the journey. We'll get you fed and warmed up, and you'll be fine."

"Thank you," he replied, taking the beer and offering his hand. "I'm James Hilton, by the way."

"John," the man replied, taking his outstretched hand in a firm grip. "John Gellie. That's my wife over there, Jenny playing in the water with our two kids."

Hilton looked up. There was a young, pretty woman, sitting on the edge of the sandy oasis, with a boy no more than five, and a baby girl in her arms. He smiled politely and said, "Cute kids."

"Thanks," John said. "Ben, my boy, just loves his baby sister, Elise."

Hilton glanced at the kids, the man's beautiful wife, and the majestic surroundings. The place looked like heaven all right. But if it was, it wasn't his heaven. He just wanted to eat, restore his strength, and get back to civilization. Somewhere he could catch a flight back to London.

John, noticing Hilton's pensive silence, said, "I'll go see if I can find you something warm to eat from the kitchen."

Hilton grinned. "Thank you. I'm famished."

"No problem."

Hilton took off his thick jacket, folding it onto the table next to him. He suppressed a wry grin, still incredulous that anywhere this high up in the Himalayan mountains could be so warm. If someone had told him he was in the middle of the Pacific Ocean along the equator, he would have found it easier to believe.

He pulled out the rudimentary map that he'd taken from the pilot. On it was a single notation of the letter "S," indicating the location of Shangri-La. The map didn't appear to be very accurate in its drawings, but from what he gathered, the lamasery was somewhere smack, bang, in the middle of the damned mountain ranges. That meant, it was going to be a long and arduous journey to reach civilization again. He would probably need to spend a few days regaining his strength before setting off.

Hilton finished the beer and took a deep breath. The sweet scent of exotic fruits and tropical flowers filled his nostrils.

He clasped his hands behind his head and sighed. *What is this place?*

John came back a little while later and offered him a plate of roast beef, with an array of delicious vegetables marinated in rosemary.

Hilton shook his head in amazement. "Thank you! That looks wonderful."

"You're welcome," John replied, pouring them both another beer.

"Thanks." Hilton took it. They clanked their glasses together. "Cheers."

Hilton took a swig and then began eating his meal. The roast was cooked to perfection and tasted divine in his mouth. He enjoyed the first bite, savoring the taste for a few seconds, before ravenously devouring the rest of it. John looked at him, his lips parted in a pleased smile. "I'm glad you're enjoying it."

"I am. Thank you."

"So where have you come from?"

"Colombo, Sri Lanka." Hilton considered where to begin. "I was on a flight to Karachi, but our aircraft was struck by lightning and the pilot had to put us down in the mountain range..."

John waited, and listened with rapt attention as Hilton filled him in on the whole, unbelievable story. When he was finished, John laughed and shook his head. Incredulity plastered across his face, he said, "You mean to tell me you literally fell into our secret lamasery?"

"Afraid so."

"Well. That's never happened before. No one's ever reached us from the Himalayan Mountains before. I wouldn't have even believed it was possible."

"Yeah, well I wouldn't recommend it. So how do people normally travel here?"

John opened his mouth to talk, but paused – as though considering how much he should say, if anything at all. "Look. You really shouldn't be here. You don't belong."

Hilton laughed at that. "You bet I don't belong here. Just let me recover my strength and I'll be on my way."

"What is this place?" Hilton asked, sweeping the utopia with his eyes. It was like no spiritual place of worship he'd ever seen. His eyes glanced at the few other people that could be seen. The men wore Hawaiian shirts and swimming shorts, while the women wore flowery dresses. One thing was certain. They sure as heck weren't monks seeking everlasting enlightenment. "I mean, it's not like any lamasery I've ever seen."

The small creases around John's mouth deepened. He appeared torn, as though he wanted to tell him as a reward for having reached the place, but it was forbidden. His indecision broke and in a whispered voice, he said, "It's a type of sanctuary."

"I'll say. Some sanctuary. It's a tropical paradise high in the Himalayan Mountains!" Hilton grinned. "What are you trying to achieve protection from?"

"Each other."

A wry grin formed on Hilton's lips. "You travel all the way out here to seek sanctuary from each other?"

John nodded his head. "That's about the gist of it."

"Seems like a colossal waste to me. I mean, why bother coming here together at all?"

"Because it's a sanctuary for us."

"Right... I understand..." Hilton said in such a way that suggested it made anything but sense to him. "I mean, why bother coming here at all? Why not just go somewhere else?"

"Look. I'm going to let you in on a little secret, but you can't ever tell anyone. And I know you won't, because, even if you did, no one would ever believe you."

The journalist in Hilton said, "Go on."

John brought his hands together, steepling his fingers. "Imagine the most powerful people in the world... can you do that?"

"Sure," Hilton said, happy to play along.

"You probably see politicians. There's an image in your head right now of Herbert Hoover pulling the levers of economics to save the US economy from the Great Depression. You see Prime Minister Ramsay MacDonald speaking with His Majesty King George the 5th. You'd see prominent CEOs who wield the power of nations. Am I right? Is that what you see?"

"Yeah. That sounds about right."

"If you believe that, then we've pulled the wool over your eyes, too."

Hilton was incredulous. "I'm wrong?"

"Yes, but if it makes you feel better, so is everyone else."

"So who wields the power?"

"We do. The puppeteers. We pull the strings that control those who think they have all the power."

Hilton didn't bother to ask how they achieved it, but instead asked, "Why?"

"Picture this… a battle of good versus evil is currently raging. In fact, it's been raging throughout the ages, and our purpose is to make sure the side of reason endures."

"But none of you get along?"

"It's not as simple as that…" John's voice trailed off into hushed tones and he stopped speaking.

Another guest glanced at Hilton. The man had pale white skin like a ghost and seemed to fixate on Hilton's brown eyes as though there was something abjectly wrong with them. It was only then that Hilton noticed John and the other guest both had dark violet eyes.

The newcomer said, "You don't belong here."

"Excuse me?" Hilton replied.

"How the hell did you get in here?"

"I um… I kind of fell…"

The newcomer licked his lips. "I'll say…"

The man turned to John. His tone admonishing. "He doesn't belong here. He shouldn't be here."

"It's all right," John said. "I was just sending him on his way."

"He shouldn't be allowed to leave. He might tell others," the newcomer warned.

John folded his arms across his chest. "Who would believe him?"

"I don't know, but I don't like it."

Hilton stood up, realizing there was going to be trouble. "It's all right, I'm leaving. Just point me in the right direction, and I'll go."

John said, "Come with me. I'll show you."

The newcomer stood up. His voice raised, just slightly. "I don't like this. I'd better get the Caretaker."

John dismissed him with the wave of his hand. "It's all right Haddock. He's going…"

"No he's not. We won't let him," Haddock said, shaking his head, before making a bee-line for a small building toward the end of the lamasery.

John didn't wait for him to return. "Come on. We'd better be quick."

Hilton didn't need to be told twice. "Agreed. Get me out of here!"

They ran past the oasis of fresh, crystal clear water, all the way back to the dark cave from which Hilton had arrived. There were two openings. One with a void that headed upward to wherever Hilton had fallen, and the other one on the opposite side, with a void below that disappeared into the Earth.

John headed to the second cave.

The one with the seemingly endless abyss.

John stopped at the engraved section of the cave and inserted a medallion that looked identical to the one Hilton had been given by the pilot of the Avro 652. The bronze-copper metal suddenly turned gold. There were eight markings that lit up along the outer edge of the medallion. It was the first time Hilton had noticed them.

Hilton stared at it, mesmerized and dumbfounded.

John said, "Quick! We don't have much time. Where do you want to go?"

"Anywhere. I just need to reach civilization so I can get a flight home."

"Where's that?"

"London."

"Right."

"Right… what?"

John spun the medallion until it stopped at one of the eight markers, and then said, "Step into the cave."

Hilton took a breath. "Wait… are you kidding me? I can't step in there. It's nothing but an endless void. There's no way to tell where it will end. I'll probably fall to my death!"

John said, "You don't have much time! Go now!"

Hilton turned his head to see a group of five people running to meet him. They didn't carry any sort of weapons, but they didn't look happy either. There was something about them that gave him the impression of a mob just about to string him up.

"Hilton!" John's words were fierce and emphatic. "Get in the damned cave. They'll never let you leave here alive!"

Hilton turned. In a muffled voice, he said, "Yeah… I think I'd better take my chances."

He looked into the cave, where a few seconds earlier there was nothing but an empty void. The void was gone, and in its place, rested a solid ground of black, glistening obsidian. It was shaped so perfectly that it was impossible to tell where the flooring ended and the rounded walls began.

His eyes narrowed. "What is this place?"

John pushed him inside.

Hilton planted his feet on the ground. Reassured that the floor was real. He looked back at his benefactor.

An instant later the floor gave way.

He tried to jump out, but he was a split second too late. And he entered a free fall that felt like it would never stop.

*

Oak Hill Gardens, North London – 1933

James Hilton woke up in a heavy sweat.

His heart raced, and a sense of impending doom filled his very being. In the back of his ears the sound of blood echoed. He was having another panic attack. They were getting worse. Always at 4 a.m. Every single damned day. It had been two years since he'd stumbled across Shangri-La – the worst mistake in his life.

He switched on his bedside light.

The room took minimalism at its word. It consisted of a single bed, a plain wooden desk, and a *Rag and Bone* typewriter. Just the way he liked it. No distractions. Hilton knew there was only one treatment for what he had. He had to get the story out of his head. He needed to finish what he'd begun. It was the only way to save himself.

He rolled out of bed and continued typing.

The story flowed quickly from where he had left off only hours earlier. He worked with the sort of focus that bordered on clinical obsession. He beat at the keys, ravenously hammering out the words, before it was too late.

He worked all day, stopping only briefly for a sandwich and an occasional cigar. When he was finished, he reread some of the prominent sections.

Shangri-La isn't just a utopic destination. It's a waterhole in the vast desert of Earth. It's a sanctuary for travelers. A place where great puppeteers can come to wait out their time. And time… it appears, passes very slowly for those inside Shangri-La.

He got to the end of the page and paused.

Outside he heard a sound of someone playing with the lock on the door. He turned to see who it was, and the door opened.

It was John Gellie. The man who had saved him from those who would see him killed in Shangri-La. The man was carrying a hand pistol and was already pointing it at him.

Hilton raised his hands. "What is it?"

John said, "You know, Mr. Hilton… that's a remarkable story… but you can't tell it."

James Hilton frowned. "Why not?"

"Because a lot of people will die if you do."

"This has been my life's work for the past two years!"

"And I'm sure it's great work too… but some things will need to be changed to protect the truth…"

Hilton stared at a world globe… at all the places he'd travelled…

He returned his attention to his typewriter.

Under the location's heading… he entered: *Xianggelila, China.*

John nodded. A brief smile forming on his parted lips. "Much appreciated."

Hilton sighed. "It wasn't like I had a choice, did I?"

The man shrugged as if he didn't care. Ignoring the question, he said, "Great… so have you got a name for this book?"

"Yeah, I think so…"

James Hilton grinned and typed the words, *Lost Horizons…*

Chapter One

**British Natural History Museum, London – 10 p.m.
Present Day**

The gunshot cracked and the bullet hissed through the air.

Sam Reilly ducked down, taking cover behind a five-foot-tall specimen of amethyst. Its purple crystals formed a bullet proof barrier that enveloped him like a half-cocoon. He worked hard to catch his breath through pursed lips. The shots went quiet and, in the distance, he heard the casual sound of a single person's footsteps slowly moving toward him.

For a split second, he thought the round had missed.

It hadn't.

Sam glanced at his waist. Blood was beginning to spread like an incoming tide, where a bullet wound originated just left of his umbilicus. Adrenaline raged in his body, blocking out any sense of pain. *Is all that blood mine?* he wondered irrationally.

Pain hadn't registered yet. His brain, functioning like the biological supercomputer that evolution had made it, shut out the pain along with a series of other questions that needed answering, but not now.

Who was trying to kill him?

Why were they trying to kill him?

Was his wound mortal?

None of the questions mattered at the moment.

He needed to survive.

Sam tried to mentally picture his place in the museum. He'd been there before, but it had been years ago and collections along with layouts were changing all the time. Right now, he was at the Earth's Treasury level on the top floor of the museum's red zone. He'd come up through the *Earth's Crust* – a cool escalator that had taken him from the ground floor all the way up to the second through the inner core of the *Earth's Crust* – but he didn't even know where the downward escalator started. If he could get to the bottom of it, he might just be able to escape out to the street. But even that seemed unlikely. There was very little in the way of concealment or cover once he was outside.

The footsteps neared. He needed to move. His eyes darted to the crest of a nearby Styrofoam volcano to his right that was a little taller than he was. It wouldn't offer much in the way of protection, but it might conceal his movements – and more importantly, it was his only option.

Sam made the move immediately.

He bolted across the floor, and dived over the volcano, sending millions of tiny Styrofoam balls into the air. He crashed down on the opposite side and skirted past the glistening display cabinet of precious and semi-precious gemstones and the sign that suggested all these wonders came from the intense heat and pressure of a volcano. Following him, came the raspy sounds of silenced shots being fired overhead.

Glass shattered everywhere and he dived around the corner and into the *Earth's Crust* escalator. The upward moving escalator shared a set of stairs which ran parallel. The stairs and escalator were split by a one-foot thick, stainless steel divider. Sam landed on the divider, sliding down like a kid on a slide at an amusement park.

He descended both floors at break-neck speed, landing hard on both feet at the bottom. Behind him, his pursuer followed him down the stairway, taking three steps at a time. Sam weaved around the corner just as his attacker took another shot.

This one went wide.

Sam turned to the right, leaving the red zone and entering the green zone. He jumped over a fossilized crocodile, before sliding through a hollowed out giant sequoia tree. He passed a temporary display of early Neanderthals, grabbing a small 160,000-year-old hand axe in the process without stopping. It had an Acheulean head of flint, set in the distinctive oval and pear-shape, which had been glued to the haft with a viscous tar distilled from birch bark.

It felt good to have a weapon.

Albeit a primitive one.

Sam kept running. Behind him, he could hear the sound of heavy breathing and footsteps being planted at speed, as his assailant continued pursuit.

Sam's chest burned with exhaustion. He was still losing blood and there was no way he could keep outrunning his attacker. He needed to even the playing field. He needed to bring things in close and confined.

Somewhere his Neanderthal hand axe could have a chance.

He crossed the Hintze Hall, with its grand entrance way, soaring Romanesque arches and magnificent stone staircase beneath the skeletal remains of a Blue Whale and dropped down into the blue zone, where dinosaurs filled the room from floor to ceiling. In the middle of the room was the skeletal remains of a massive dinosaur head – most likely a T-Rex – its teeth bared in a deadly grin.

On the far side of the room, Sam jumped a barrier and entered the control room, which housed the complex web of wires that were responsible for maneuvering and supporting the overhead exhibits.

Behind him, the footsteps turned silent.

"You might as well come out now," said a confident female voice. "I can see where you've gone. It's not hard. You're leaving one hell of a blood trail. I doubt I still even need to finish my job. You're trapped, so come on out, and I'll make this quick for you."

Sam held his breath and crouched down with his back against the wall. She was right. There was nowhere else for him to go. He'd reached a dead end. She knew where he was, and even if she didn't, he was bleeding to death. Already, he was starting to struggle to see, his vision was blurred, and he was ready to pass out at any moment.

Along the wall were more than a hundred thin wires leading toward the hanging displays on the ceiling. There was no telling which one led to which exhibit. But maybe he might cause a diversion somehow.

He brought the Neanderthal hand-axe back, and gave it a hard swing. The force came from his powerful shoulders and the flint head sliced straight through four wires in one go. Sam didn't wait to see if he'd caused any damage. Instead, he swung the axe again and again.

Nothing happened.

Then, a moment later, the wires began to race through their running lines.

Outside he heard the woman cry out, before the sound was drowned out by the shattering of a very large exhibit falling to the ground.

Sam didn't wait for a second chance.

He forced himself to stand and climbed out of the control room.

And stopped.

There, halfway across the room, was his assailant. Her entire body crushed by the head of a prehistoric T-Rex. Sam Reilly picked up his cell phone and dialed 999.

The operator asked, "Police, Fire, or Ambulance."

Sam gasped. "Ambulance… I've been shot!"

A moment later, his eyes blurred, his vision waned, and his eyes, wide open, saw nothing but darkness…

Chapter Two

Tom Bower pressed the starter button.

The green Kawasaki ZX-10R SE came to life. Its inline 1000 cc engine produced a resonant and smooth purr. He quickly typed the address for *Chelsea and Westminster Hospital* into his phone's satnav and placed it on the motorcycle's dash.

His eyes narrowed on the route.

It didn't look too far, but the roads in London were notoriously busy even this late at night. He pulled in the clutch, kicked his left foot down on the gear lever, sliding the gear into first, gave the throttle a little bit of power, and released the clutch.

The motorcycle responded like the weapon it was made to be. Accelerating quickly along *Tower Bridge Road.* On his right, he passed the medieval Tower of London, and weaved in and out of traffic, as he crossed the *Tower Bridge.*

The bike responded well to his inputs. It would have been a fun bike to ride under their original arrangement.

Not that they'd get to still do their original plan.

They had hired the bikes to join a group of cave divers for a project in Scotland and had decided to make a riding vacation out of it.

How quickly things change.

Ten minutes earlier, he was about to settle down for the night, when Sam had called to say he'd been shot and was on his way to *Chelsea and Westminster Hospital.* By the sounds of things, he'd lost a lot of blood and wasn't very well at all. In typical Sam Reilly fashion, he was adamant that it was imperative Tom reached him before he went under anesthetic. Something about receiving something he needed Tom to have – and as per usual, it was a matter of life and death.

He didn't know much about what had happened yet. Just that there was a major incident at the British Museum of Natural History. The curator had been shot dead and Sam Reilly had been shot and sustained life-threatening injuries.

Tom brought the bike up to 80 miles an hour as he swung round to the west, crossing the *Thames* via the *Vauxhall Bridge*. He brought the bike up to a near-stop, before cutting in front of a lorry and headed south along *Grosvenor Road.*

He hugged the river for a few miles before pulling into the *Chelsea and Westminster Hospital* ambulance bay.

An ambulance was just parking.

Tom pulled the motorcycle to the edge of a parking bay and got off.

A paramedic opened the back door to the ambulance and pulled the gurney out.

At a glance, Sam Reilly looked terrible. He was ashen gray, and small beads of sweat had formed on his forehead. He had an oxygen mask on his face and two cannulas in his arms, which were being fed by some sort of bag of fluid.

Tom didn't need to be a paramedic to know Sam was shutting down.

One of the paramedics spotted him. "You're Tom Bower?"

"Yes, sir."

"Good. You can come with us while they get him up to surgery. He's refusing to go under until he speaks with you."

The trauma surgeon in charge met them at the door, trying to get as much medical history from Sam as he could on the way to surgery.

Tom nodded and followed them as they wheeled Sam into the hospital. He gripped Sam's hand. "Hey, how are you doing?"

"I'm all right. How was your ride?"

"Good." Tom arched an eyebrow. His friend was clearly dying, but he wanted to know how the bike ran under speed. He returned to the problem in hand. "You said you had to give me something?"

Sam removed a USB stick from his pocket and handed it to him. "Get this to Elise right away! Don't wait until the morning. She needs to see what's on it, now!"

"I'm sorry, sir," the surgeon said. "We need to start the anesthetic if we're going to have a chance to stem this bleeding before you die."

Sam nodded. "Do what you need to do, doc."

Tom looked at the USB stick. "What's on it?"

Sam cut him off with a dismissive wave of his hand. "Just find Elise. She'll know exactly what to do."

Chapter Three

Jodhpur, Rajasthan – India

Elise closed the car door and watched the yellow Toyota Innova Crysta pull away. Her gaze turned to the sprawling city of Jodhpur. The city was a popular tourist destination, featuring many palaces, forts and temples, set in the stark landscape of the Thar Desert.

The afternoon sun shone down across the intricate web of high-density houses, sending long shadows over the complex puzzle of adjoining low-lying building all set together in a chaotic and fractured example of early Rajasthan town planning. Thousands of alleyways intermingled to form a maze. The houses in the old city were typically painted in a blue, giving rise to the city's nickname, the "Blue City."

Rising majestically from the center was the Mehrangarh Fort.

The 15th century fortress was situated 410 feet above the city and enclosed by imposing thick walls of stone, some 118 feet high and 69 feet wide. The Khandwaliya community, one of the oldest traditional communities in India, had knowledge of breaking the big stones that made this fort using technology that others had long since forgotten.

Ben Gellie met her eye. "It's quite remarkable, isn't it?"

Elise nodded. "Yeah. Stunning."

Ben fed his arms through the shoulder straps of his backpack, pulling the chest strap tight. "Let's keep going. We need to reach the museum just after it closes."

Elise took the weight of her backpack and started walking. "You set the pace and I'll match it."

They headed due west, through the obtuse maze of roadways. Elise and Ben were siblings, but had been raised separately. Neither one knowing the other existed until recently. They had been told their parents had died in a car crash when they were very little. It was a sad story. No relatives had survived. Elise had grown up feeling this terrible loss. Only, the story was never true. Her parents hadn't died in a car crash, they were still alive, and they had separated their two children to keep them safe.

They had an IQ off the charts and shared identical purple eyes – a rare, genetic marker of an ancient race of people known as Master Builders.

But that was where their similarities ended.

Elise was slightly shorter than the average American woman, with a slim, and athletic figure. She had a striking face, with delicate, partially Eurasian features, golden skin, and light brown hair. She wore a loose-fitting shirt, revealing a narrow waste, with toned, muscular arms.

Ben, on the other hand, was tall – just above six foot – clean-shaven, and wore a polo shirt over a pair of jeans. His skin was tan, but Caucasian with no evidence of any Asian ancestry. He had handsome boyish good looks, and thick, wavy hair.

Three weeks ago, Ben had approached her out of the blue, and informed her that not only had her parents never been in a car crash when they were kids, but that they were still alive. Their parents were currently taking refuge in a place called Shangri-La. It was because of that near mythical lamasery, that the two had come to Jodhpur today.

They followed a winding road that led from the city below all the way to the base of the Mehrangarh Fort. The imprints of the impact of cannonballs fired by attacking armies could still be seen on the second gate. To the left of the fort is the chhatri of Kirat Singh Soda, a soldier who fell on the spot defending the Mehrangarh Fort.

They entered the fort through a series of seven gates, the second of which, showed the imprints of the impact of cannonballs fired by attacking armies. To their left, they passed the chhatri of Kirat Singh Soda. The elevated, dome-shaped pavilion, a common element in Indian architecture, paid respects to a soldier who fell on the spot defending the Mehrangarh Fort.

Inside its boundaries there were several palaces known for their intricate carvings and expansive courtyards.

Ben walked quickly and confidently, as though he'd been to the place before, or at least knew its layout well beforehand. They walked against the tide of tourists leaving the UNESCO World Heritage Site.

Ben stopped outside the entrance to the Mehrangarh Museum.

A security guard stepped out to greet them. He was tall, with a slim build, and a hard face. The man shook Ben's hand. "Mr. Gellie?"

"Yes, and this is my sister, Elise."

The guard turned to Elise. "Welcome to Mehrangarh."

"Thank you," she replied, before saying with genuine respect, "The fort looks amazing."

"Yes, it is. My great ancestors built this in ways that have defied modern science." The guard opened the door, and parted the palm of his hand outward. "Please, after you."

Ben and Elise walked through into the main foyer of the historic museum.

The guard took a seat in his fishbowl shaped security office, lined with live video feeds of every room in the museum.

They left their backpacks with the security guard and Ben paid the man the price of an after hour, self-guided admission – a small handful of 2,000 Indian Rupee notes.

The guard took it, struggling to suppress his grin. It was more than his entire annual salary. "Thank you, Mr. Gellie. I hope you enjoy the museum."

Ben replied, "I'm sure we will."

The guard pressed a button and the main entrance door digitally unlocked. "Oh, one more thing…"

Ben turned to meet him. "Yes?"

"Be sure not to touch anything." The guard pointed to the array of computer monitors that displayed each room of the museum. "Everything is recorded. If something goes missing, no bribe will make me look the other way."

"Understood," Ben replied. Then, with a you-can-trust-me kind of smile, he said, "We just want to have the opportunity to inspect your rich history without the masses."

"Very good, my friend. Enjoy."

"We will," Ben said, and then for the benefit of keeping up their pretense, he said, "We're going to start at the end, looking at the greatest treasures, and then work our way back."

Chapter Four

Elise ran her eyes across the museum, getting her bearings.

The grand rooms were marbled with large sweeping archways, intricately carved with historical features. Ben had done his job. It was time for her to play her part. She followed the passageway to the left.

Inside were a series of Elephant Howdahs, a kind of two-compartment wooden seat, heavily gilded in gold and silver embossed sheets, which were then able to be fastened onto the elephant's back. The front compartment, with more leg space and a raised protective metal sheet, was meant for kings or royalty, and the rear smaller one for a reliable bodyguard disguised as a fly-whisk attendant.

She casually glanced over a set of palanquins and kept walking. A series of windows revealed the city of Jodhpur, a constellation of small lights turning a sharp contrast against the darkness of night. Elise smiled, slowing her stride for a moment, and pointed out at the city. It was a practiced response, and certainly more what the security guard would be expecting – assuming he was indeed going to watch their every movement from the comfort of his security control room.

They kept going. Ben following just behind her as they entered the armory. Ben paused, with what appeared to be genuine pleasure, as he took in the gallery's displays of armor from every period in Jodhpur. On display were sword hilts in jade, silver, rhino horn, ivory, shields studded with rubies, emeralds and pearls and guns with gold and silver work on the barrels. The gallery also had on display the personal swords of many emperors, among them outstanding historical pieces.

Elise turned to the left, taking in a series of Marwar-Jodhpur paintings, before entering the Turban gallery, which displayed the many different types of turbans once prevalent in Rajasthan – with every community, region, and festival having had its own head-gear.

At last they reached what she was after…

The Daulat Khana – Treasures of Mehrangarh Museum.

Inside the final gallery were a series of displays that housed the most important and best-preserved collections of fine and applied arts of the Mughal period of Indian history, during which the Rathore rulers of Jodhpur maintained close links with the Mughal emperors. It also has the remains of Emperor Akbar and a dedication to the founder of the Mehrangarh, Rao Jodha.

Elise and Ben stopped beside the featured display of Rao Jodha, who founded the city of Jodhpur in 1459. Everything was protected by a heavy glass security case. There was a tunic, turban, and series of personal artifacts. To the side of which, was a small, heavily tarnished, bronze-colored medallion. It didn't look particularly valuable and the two circular emblems once intricately carved into the metal appeared worn and barely visible.

Elise grinned. "There it is."

"Yes." Ben exhaled slowly, speaking almost reverently, "There it is." She took a slow walk around the glass security cabinet. The only access was through a thick, glass door, which was sealed by a magnetic lock. It required a digital pass to open. The device used a surprisingly rudimentary security code, something she could break within minutes once she got going. But the real problem was doing so while the cameras watched.

This is where Ben came in.

He came and stood next to her, shielding her from the camera's view.

She placed her code-breaking device up against the pass. The system ran a program, based on an algorithm that she had designed, that looks at every possible digital code, and offers every single one simultaneously. In a more complex security system, the pass would receive all the attempted passcodes and the program would determine it was under attack.

But the Mehrangarh used a decidedly lower budget for security, its curator most likely assuming that given nothing was of any intrinsic value inside, only historical value, it was unlikely to be targeted by highly organized cyber criminals.

The card beeped, and the door opened.

From inside her pocket she removed a medallion. The replica was visually identical to the one inside the display cabinet. Identical to the naked eye. Yes, one was extremely valuable and one was nothing more than a weathered bronze medallion.

It was now a matter of sleight of hand.

And like all good magicians, this needed a distraction.

Beside them, was a life-sized, hand crafted display of each of the early Mughal emperors. Ben leaned on one, knocking it over, so that it fell with a loud clanging sound.

Elise opened the glass door and in a split second replaced the replica medallion for the real thing, closing the door an instant afterward. The lock made a slight beep sound as it sealed shut again. And within thirty seconds, the security guard was upon them.

Ben put his hand up. "I'm sorry. I don't know what happened. I just tripped. I'll pay for that, I promise!"

The guard looked at him, his eyes narrow and scrutinizing. There was a determined mixture of anger and fear, dished out in equal proportions. The man's face vacillated between his need to punish Ben for his carelessness, but also his desire not to reveal that he had let people into the museum after hours.

The guard asked, "Did you touch anything else?"

"No. Just this." Ben said, with a half-shrug of his shoulders, holding the palms of his hands outward in an apology. "Like I said, if anything's broken, I'm happy to pay for it."

The guard appeared placated. "No, no... let's see if we can stand this model up again."

The entire mannequin was made of metal and fabric. It was heavy, but tough. Once it was upright, the guard examined it for any breakages.

He exhaled a sigh of relief. "It looks like it's your lucky day. Nothing is broken."

"That's great," Ben said, taking an apologetic tone bordering on obsequiousness. "I am so sorry."

The guard caught Elise's eyes dart toward the glass case. One of the artifacts – a jade pendant hanging across Rao Jodha's neck – appeared to be swinging ever so slightly, as though someone had knocked it.

For the first time, the guard suddenly wondered whether or not something might actually have been stolen. He moved on Elise with surprising speed. "What did you do?"

"Nothing! Nothing... I swear it."

The guard ran his eyes across the Rao Jodha exhibit, scrutinizing for anything missing. "Nothing? Why is that pendant swinging?"

Elise bit her lower lip and shrugged. "I don't know. I guess when Ben knocked over the mannequin it must have caused enough vibration to shift it."

The guard's lips hardened into a straight line. "You don't expect me to believe that, do you?"

"I don't know what you would believe or not, but it's the truth. Heck, I don't even know how you even get inside the display cabinet."

The guard's focus turned to the locked door. He gave the door a firm pull, trying to open it. The door held fast. It was locked and without a digital key, no one was going to open it.

He smiled and exhaled. "Very well. I think we can all agree that the night museum is now shut."

Elise feigned disappointment. "But I haven't seen the turban gallery yet. Can we just have another few minutes to take a look?"

The guard set his arms across his chest in defiance. "I'm afraid absolutely not."

Elise began to argue that they'd paid for a night time visit, but Ben interrupted. "I understand. We thank you for letting us in. We'll leave now. I'm so sorry about the accident."

"That's okay. But please, I really must ask you to leave."

They followed the guard back to the security control room and retrieved their backpacks. After thanking the guard, he opened the front door and let them out.

Elise and Ben took a leisurely stroll down to the room in a hotel that they had booked. As soon as they were inside, Elise locked the door and retrieved the medallion.

Ben said, "I can't believe we have one of the last remaining medallions."

She exhaled. "I know. We're really going to see our parents."

The bathroom door opened up at the end of the room and a man with a red cap greeted them with a leveled handgun.

The man's lips curved upward into a malicious smile. "So, you want to visit Shangri-La, do you?"

Chapter Five

Tom Bower frowned as the call went straight to Elise's voicemail.

It was unlike her not to pick up. Only a handful of people had her cell number. She kept it on her at all times, and despite possibly being anywhere in the world, she was almost always reachable. It had been more than an hour since he'd tried the first time.

He sent Elise a text message.

Call me back as soon as you get this. Sam's been shot. He's in surgery now. He's given me a USB stick which he says you will know what to do with.

A couple seconds later, his phone rang.

He picked it up. "Elise!"

"No, its Margaret," the US Secretary of Defense said, dropping any sign of her usual crisp, formality. "I heard Sam Reilly was shot."

"I'm afraid so, Madam Secretary."

"Will he survive?"

"He's in surgery now. The doctors say he's lost a lot of blood, but they're hopeful they can save him. We'll find out when they finish the operation."

The Secretary showed no emotion. "What do we know about the shooting?"

"Very little. This wasn't a random mugging. He was attacked by a professional assassin at the British Natural History Museum."

"She can't be that professional if she let him live."

"Sam Reilly's not the easiest man to kill."

"So he keeps telling me." The Secretary's voice was casual and matter of fact. "He's just a person like anyone else. Luck runs out. Well placed bullets don't leave much to chance. Okay, what else do we know?"

"Not much. He was shot around 10 p.m."

"What was he doing at the museum at that time of the night?"

"He didn't say. I was catching up on rest before heading to Scotland tomorrow. He didn't mention he was ducking out to take in the sights for a private tour at the Natural History Museum!"

"Who opened up for him?"

"The curator of maritime archeology exhibit." Tom paused, thinking about anything he'd missed. "There's something else, too. Before Sam was put under for surgery, he gave me a USB stick he'd been given, and said that Elise would know what to do about it."

The pitch of her voice became inflected with curiosity. "What's on the USB stick?"

"I don't know yet. I haven't been able to get into contact with Elise. I'll put it into my laptop when I get back to the hotel and let you know if I find anything that sheds some light on our situation."

"Please do. Now, what about the curator? Surely she must be able to tell you something."

Tom sighed. "She might, if she was still alive."

"They got her, too?"

"Afraid so."

"Okay. I'll put out some feelers through official channels and see what I can find. Take care of yourself Tom and let me know if you find anything of interest on that USB stick."

"Yes, ma'am."

She ended the call and Tom went to talk to one of the nursing staff about the operation. The nurse, a man in his fifties with a trim beard, advised him the operation could go for another hour or two, and even after that it would be some time before Sam Reilly was awake in ICU. It would probably be for the best if Tom went home for the night and came back in the morning. Tom agreed and returned to the hotel.

Once there he switched on his laptop, sat down, and plugged in the USB stick.

There was only a single document inside. The folder was labeled: Xianggelila

Tom frowned. The name looked Chinese, but meant nothing to him. Next to the name was an image. It looked like a coin, or possibly a medallion made of bronze. The coin was old and tarnished. It didn't look valuable. Instead, it was more like something that had been left to the elements for years. On its face stood two circles linked together to form the symbol for infinity. Although, the more he looked at it he realized that wasn't quite right either. The circles were more than that. Instead of being a figure eight laid on its side, it was two distinctly different circles placed side-by-side. Each one depicting a snake biting its tail. There was something about it that made him think of Egypt, although why he felt that way, he couldn't tell.

He made a mental note to return to the image, and double clicked on the folder. It opened a typed list of nearly a hundred World War II era shipwrecks, along with their date of sinking, class and cargo, and GPS coordinates of their gravesites.

What the hell do the Chinese want with a list of early World War II era shipwrecks?

He typed the Xianggelila into a search engine and clicked translate.

The lines across his face deepened with disbelief as the translation was displayed on his screen:

Shangri-La.

Chapter Six

Tom returned to the list of World War II era shipwrecks. There were roughly a hundred on the list, but only eight had been highlighted with an asterisk.

His eyes swept across the names of the highlighted shipwrecks, following the order of their reference.

HMAS Perth – Australian Modified Leander Class Battleship.

Hr. M.s 0-16 – Dutch Submarine

USS Houston – United States of America Heavy Cruiser.

HMS Repulse – British Battlecruiser.

HMS Prince of Wales – British Battleship

Chosa Maru – Japanese gunboat.

Sagiri – Japanese Destroyer.

HMS Exeter – British Heavy Cruiser.

Tom shook his head and bit his lower lip. There was a spread of Australian, American, British, Dutch, and Japanese naval ships. The only similarities being they were all sunk before the end of the second world war.

What the hell do eight World War II era shipwrecks have to do with Shangri-La?

He put the list of names into a search engine and each of their locations came up on a map. They were spread out in a tight-knit grid, spread across the South China Sea, Java Sea, and the Sunda Strait. Tom glanced at the neighboring countries, trying to picture the naval battles that must have unfolded during World War II. Thailand, Cambodia, and Vietnam to the north. Malaysia, Singapore, and East Java to the east and south. With Brunei and Indonesia to the west with the Java Sea in the middle.

Tom stared at each of the ship's locations.

What do you all have in common?

He began putting each name into a search engine and scrolling through the array of articles, ranging from the vessel's development, history, sinking, and discovery. Each ship had its own story, its own history. There were intimate details of heroic deeds, while sailors from four different countries battled to survive.

There was nothing that linked them together. The only similarities the eight shipwrecks shared was the fact that they were all sunk early in World War II; whereas, the majority of the rest of the ships had been sunk after 1945.

Tom frowned. It was a connection, but tenuous at best.

What difference did a couple years make out of more than seventy-five spent dilapidating at the bottom of the ocean?

Tom decided to start at the beginning again.

He typed *HMAS Perth* into a search engine and then matched it with recent news articles. Several pages of articles came up, mostly referencing the ship's history and the battle in which it was sunk in 1942.

Tom's eyes landed on a single article that caught his attention.

Death by a Thousand Cuts

He clicked on the link and began to read the opening paragraph.

The shipwreck of HMAS Perth (I) lies in waters between Java and Sumatra, a victim of the Battle of Sunda Strait in 1942. A joint survey project between the museum and Pusat Penelitian Arkeologi Nasional (Indonesia) has recorded the devastation caused by extensive illegal salvage.

He read further, and found that the ship which had survived mostly intact for more than seventy years on the bottom of the seabed had now recently been lost to an illegal salvage operation by commercial divers, looking to extract its steel, copper, aluminum, and lead.

Tom licked his lips.

Why would anyone want to go to the trouble of salvaging metals from a World War II shipwreck?

He scrolled down to the end of the article and noted the author – a Doctor James Hunter – a maritime archeologist from the Australian Maritime Museum in Sydney.

Tom glanced at the name. Doctor *James Hunter*. He smiled. *Hunter…* a good name for a maritime archeologist, he figured.

He searched for the man's contact details. Found them, entered them into his cell, and made the call.

Chapter Seven

The man picked up on the first ring. "Hello?"

"Dr. James Hunter?" Tom asked.

"Speaking," the man replied, his voice warm and convivial.

"Doctor Hunter, my name is Tom Bower. We met a few years ago at the Australian Maritime Archeology conference in Brisbane. You were giving a talk about a submarine you were searching for. The *HMAS A...* something..."

"*HMAS AE1!*" Hunter replied, finishing it for him. "We found it off the Duke of York Islands in Papua New Guinea."

"That's right, congratulations," Tom said, waiting for the man to make the connection, when he didn't, Tom said, "I'm a colleague of Sam Reilly."

"Ah, that Tom Bower!" Hunter said, recognition in his voice. "You and Sam were giving a talk about the discovery of the Mahogany Ship."

"That's right. You have a good memory." Tom could hear the sound of a wave lapping on the hull of a ship in the background. He smiled. "Where are you?"

"Off the coast of Rhode Island. We're surveying a shipwreck we believe might be the final resting place of the *HMS Endeavor*. You actually just caught me. I was about to make a dive. But I can hold off a little while longer."

"Thank you. I really appreciate it."

Hunter said, "No problem. How is Sam? You know we go back a long way?"

Tom suppressed the pain that rose in his throat. "Actually, he's seen better days."

"What, is he sick?"

"No, he got shot."

Hunter's voice sunk. "Seriously?"

"Afraid so, he's in surgery now. Actually, that's kind of what I've called you about. I need your help."

"Really?" Hunter asked without concealing his surprise. "I'm happy to assist, but I wonder what I can possibly do to help. I mean, I'm not that sort of doctor."

"No, you're exactly the sort of doctor we need."

"Okay, tell me what you need."

And so, Tom filled him in about the list of early World War II era shipwrecks.

Chapter Eight

Tom listened as Dr. James Hunter explained the strange phenomenon.

"It's a Malaysian group, we believe have financial backers in China," Dr. Hunter said. "The salvage firms are working with an international syndicate to plunder sunken wartime wrecks in search for rare steel."

Tom asked, "How do they do that?"

"There's a variety of methods depending on the location and depths of the wreckages. Some use commercial divers to remove individual pieces of material piece by piece, others use a grab dredger or crane barge to 'fish' parts of the wreckage from the seabed."

"Sounds like a lot of work for little reward."

"Not as slow as you might think." Hunter chortled. "A crane lowers the magnet to grab metal from the rusted wrecks, which can be stripped easily in just eight hours. They then sail back into privately-owned jetties on the Selangor and Perak coasts to sort out their loot in makeshift junkyards."

"How do they get rid of it?"

"These temporary junkyards are also their worksites, used to cut up larger pieces. The sorted metal is then taken to a legitimate junkyard, where it is packed or compacted before being sent to China. There, it is melted down for reuse."

"What about the bigger projects?"

Tom asked, "Why don't the authorities hunt down all the vessels involved in the illegal salvage activities?"

"They've tried. Like the drug trade, they catch some, but most slip through their nets."

"How come?"

"The vessels, dredges and barges used in the operation may be registered to different owners. None are anchored at the same location at any one time. The ships, mostly captained by Chinese nationals with a dozen or so foreign crew, are spread across the Straits of Malacca, and the Java and Sunda Seas. The vessels sometimes sail for weeks without carrying out any actual salvage work, coming into port to refuel and resupply before setting out to sea again."

"If the maritime authorities know where all the shipwrecks are, can't they set a trap and lay in wait for them?"

Hunter laughed at Tom's simple solution. "If they had one gigantean budget, they might. But the reality is, it's a few naval vessels, trying to stop a massive illegal syndicate. They're all connected and they know where the authorities are at any given time. Besides, the syndicate has become very adept at avoiding maritime authorities."

"How?"

"They operate for a few hours each day and sail back out to international waters, where the authorities have no power to search or detain ships."

"Can't they search and detain the ships once they enter the various countries territorial waters?"

"Sure, but the crews pretend to be fishermen. Their vessels are like chameleons, capable of providing both services, and for all intensive purposes, appear no different than legitimate fishing boats."

Tom exhaled a deep breath, still trying to rack his brain around the operation. "Why in the world would anyone want to go to the trouble?"

"To salvage steel that's been laying at the bottom of the ocean for three quarters of a century?" Dr. Hunter asked.

Tom gave a half-shrug. "Yeah, I mean, it can't be the most cost-effective way to make steel."

Dr. Hunter sighed. "That's what makes this all the more terrifying."

"Why?"

"Because these are the last stores of steel on Earth that haven't been affected by the detonation of nuclear bombs."

Chapter Nine

Tom lips twisted into a wry smile. "They want the metal because it hasn't been disturbed by the detonation of nuclear bombs?"

"Exactly," Dr. Hunter replied. "Told you it was terrifying stuff! The illegal salvagers are scavenging steel plating made before the nuclear testing era, which filled the atmosphere with radiation. These submerged ships are one of the last sources of "low background steel," which is virtually radiation-free and vital for some scientific and medical equipment."

"Are you telling me every piece of steel on Earth currently is affected by radiation from nuclear detonation of Hiroshima and Nagasaki?"

"Afraid so, my friend."

"The nuclear radiation from two bombs filtered throughout the globe, spreading radiation which has permeated every piece of metal made ever since then?"

Hunter said, "Yes, but we're not just talking about Hiroshima and Nagasaki, are we?"

Tom replied, "We aren't?"

"No. It's a lot more than that... we'll get to it. First off, how much do you know about how steel is made?"

"Not much," Tom confided.

"Okay, let's start at the beginning. Steel is a widely used metal which is made from iron. It is considered better than iron, due to it being stronger and less brittle. The process to make steel is pretty simple. Iron ore, which is mined from the ground, contains a lot of impurities and carbon, which act to make the iron weaker. To remove these unwanted materials, the iron is heated up in a blast furnace until it becomes molten, before limestone is added to the mixture. The limestone floats on top of the molten iron and draws out the impurities and some of the excess carbon from the iron mixture." Dr. Hunter paused. "Are you still following?"

"Sure. I forget most of my high school chemistry days, but I'm keeping up."

"Good. Now, air from the atmosphere is used in the process to help remove impurities from the iron ore. These impurities are then drained away, leaving iron with a small, controlled amount of carbon in it, which we call steel. This process worked great for hundreds of years, until the 16th of July 1945 at 5:26 am. From that moment on, steel making and the world as a whole changed forever, because this was the first detonation of an atomic bomb."

Tom said, "The Trinity Test."

"You got it," Hunter said. "The trinity test, as it was known, was the first detonation of an atomic bomb and was shortly followed by the detonation of the two bombs at Hiroshima and Nagasaki which ended the second World War. Many people think that these were the only atomic weapons ever detonated. But they're wrong. There have been around 1,900 atomic weapons tests since the end of the second World War. With each of these explosions, radiation and radioactive material was released in to the world and has slowly built up over time."

"Okay, so is this background radiation killing us?"

"You mean, causing cancer?"

"Yeah."

"Probably. I don't know. Experts say its relatively low, so probably not too much. But who could really say?"

"Okay," Tom said, trying to suppress the thought of this newly discovered nightmare from his mind and concentrate on the task at hand. "Why's it so important to make low-radiation steel?"

"Glad you asked. So, let's imagine that today you wanted to build an incredibly sensitive radiation detector, such as a Geiger counter or a medical radiation scanner. To get the most accurate readings you have to make sure none of the components inside the detector are themselves radioactive, otherwise your detector will be less sensitive, and this is where our problem with modern created steel comes from. Because we pass air through iron to make steel, any radioactive particles in the air which are left over from the nearly two thousand nuclear detonations over the years will become part of the steel. This makes all modern-day steel, made using atmospheric air, slightly radioactive. This steel can't be used in any type of sensitive radiation detector, including medical scanners."

"And therein lies the solution. Salvage the steel plating of early World War II era shipwrecks, which have been protected from nuclear radiation by seawater."

"That's it. Now you're getting it. We have to use steel that was made before the first ever atomic detonation, also known as low-background steel. This means, we can only use steel that was made before the 16th of July 1945. Any steel made after this day has a chance of containing radioactive particles, splitting the history of steel in to two very distinct periods. However, back in 1945, most produced steel went in to making ships and tanks for the war effort. This makes sunken ships, which lay untouched under the ocean, one of the only reliable sources of non-radioactive steel. Being under the water has also protected the steel from being directly exposed to any radiation, as water is a very good blocker of radioactive particles and energy. As a result, when we need to make medical or physics equipment out of steel which needs to be very sensitive to radiation, we often have to use steel from sunken battleships."

Tom asked, "Any idea what makes these eight ships highlighted any more or less valuable?"

"No. None whatsoever." Dr. Hunter said, "Look, I'll talk to some colleagues of mine, see if they have any ideas, and get back to you as soon as I have some answers."

Chapter Ten

Tom was getting tired. He'd been awake for more than thirty hours now. He needed rest. He laid his head on the pillow and his cell phone began to buzz again.

He sat bolt upright and picked up it immediately, hoping it was Elise.

It wasn't.

"Tom Bower?" came a man's voice, in a soft, almost guarded manner.

"Yes?"

"This is Doctor Michael Haddock from *Chelsea and Westminster Hospital*. We met earlier tonight."

"Yes, of course, Doctor Haddock." His heart raced, and any sense of tiredness immediately left his body. He was awake now. There was something about the man's voice that sent a chill down his spine. "What is it?"

"We've completed the surgery." The surgeon paused, as though he wasn't sure if he wanted to explain the rest of it.

Tom shook his head. What is it with this guy, is he waiting for dramatic effect? "How did it go?"

"Look. That bullet nicked Sam Reilly's mesenteric artery. That's the big one in the gut. He's lost a lot of blood. We've had to replace that with a number of blood transfusions. We repaired the artery, removed the bullet, and cleaned the wound. We're not really too worried about the wound... he should be all right on that score."

"I'm sorry, Doc. This all sounds good to me, what is it you're not telling me? There's something that is obviously concerning you."

"Mr. Bower, normally after this sort of operation, one involving abdominal surgery, but no injuries to the brain, we expect the patient to wake up shortly after we stop using the anesthetic agents."

"And in Sam Reilly's case?"

"I'm afraid he's still unconscious. It's early still, but we would have expected him to wake up by now."

"What does that mean?"

"It could mean anything. The most likely explanation is that his body doesn't metabolize the anesthetic agent very well, so he's going to remain under longer than we would expect."

Tom swallowed hard. "Worst case scenario, Doc?"

The doctor expelled a breath. "He simply lost too much blood before we could operate and as a consequence, his brain didn't get enough oxygen."

"You mean…"

The doctor's voice hardened. "Sam Reilly may never wake up."

Chapter Eleven

Tom woke up feeling more tired than when he went to bed.

The weight of everything that had happened seemed oppressive, making it hard to breathe. His mind raced, replaying everything over and over again, in an attempt to find something to focus on until Sam woke up. He checked the time.

It was 6:20 a.m.

He'd been asleep for little over four hours. It wasn't much, but it was all he was going to get now that his mind was firing again.

Tom glanced at his cell phone in the hope that he'd missed a call from the hospital or Elise. He hadn't. *Where are you Elise?* The doctor had told him that Sam Reilly had been moved to the Intensive Care Unit, and Tom insisted someone call him the instant Sam showed signs of waking up. He still refused to believe this would be the end of the line for his Sam.

There wasn't anything he could do for his friend just yet. He knew he needed more rest. Four hours probably wasn't enough. They had gotten off a long-haul flight to England yesterday, and had stayed up all day to settle into the new time zone. By the time he'd gone to bed, he'd been awake for more than 32 hours. He needed more sleep, but he wasn't ready. His mind wouldn't shut down. Chewing on an unsolved problem was what he needed to get him out of his head.

Tom returned to his laptop and switched it on.

His eyes locked on the strange image of a medallion next to the document name – Xianggelila.

Staring at the bronze coin, he thought, *what are you?*

Normally, he'd send the image to Elise, who would do her computer wizardry, searching a series of global databases ranging from archeology, science, through to historical documents. But she was missing. Sam Reilly was still unconscious and he was on his own.

Tom sheepishly brought up Google.

It would have to do. He clicked on the images icon and then clicked, *search by image*. The tab opened up asking him if wanted to *upload an image* or *paste image URL*. He clicked *upload an image*.

There were no exact matches found, but hundreds of pages of similar matches. The most common match was that of a serpent eating its own tail, to form a circle around an ancient Egyptian face. He frowned. There wasn't much information about the iconography.

He scrolled through and stopped.

There, in front of him was an image – taken by a tourist – of a series of ancient Egyptian hieroglyphs found within the Great Pyramid Khufu. The hieroglyph depicted an Egyptian ruler. It looked like any other image found along the great walls inside the pyramids, with one exception. Draped from the ruler's long neck, was a medallion.

Tom's lips parted into a grin.

It was an identical match with the one that he'd seen on the USB that Sam had given him. It might even be the very same medallion.

The question remained, what did an ancient Egyptian medallion have to do with a secret plot to steal World War II shipwrecks?

Tom had no idea, but he knew someone who might.

He picked up his cell phone and made a call.

A woman answered. "You've got some nerve calling me at this time of night..."

Tom said, "Hello, Billie. Don't hang up. I need your help."

Chapter Twelve

Doctor Billie Swan was an expert in ancient Egyptology and one of the few people on Earth highly knowledgeable about the Master Builders.

But for Tom, she was always the girl who had gotten away.

They had dated for three years before Billie had broken it off so that she could pursue her research into the Master Builders. Since then, Tom and Genevieve had become an item. Despite most people's expectations, the three of them got along really well.

Tom quickly brought Billie up to speed about what had happened.

He texted her a copy of the medallion image and asked, "Have you ever seen anything like it?"

"The short answer is not really," she said. "I mean, parts of the image are based on simple iconologies, which I could break down easily enough, but there's nothing here that I can say I completely recognized."

"That's it?" Tom asked, without trying to conceal his surprise. "I expected you to have all the answers for me! You can't tell me anything?"

"Hey, I didn't say that!" There was humor and victory in her voice, teasing him. "I just said that I'd never seen anything like this medallion."

"What can you tell me?"

"Lots." Tom pictured Billie smiling triumphantly on the other end of the phone. "For starters, I can tell you this is one of the most important images I've seen for a very long time."

Tom's lips curved upward into a half-grin. "Important? In what way?"

"I'll get to that."

"Okay. What can you tell me about this infinity symbol?"

"Well, that's interesting, isn't it?" Billie said, "Although the symbol resembles a geometric figure called a lemniscate, this symbol goes back much further."

Tom's eyes narrowed on the image. "Go on."

"The shape of a sideways figure eight has a long pedigree. It appears in the cross of Saint Boniface, wrapped around the bars of a Latin cross in 752 A.D. Mathematician, John Wallis is credited with introducing the infinity symbol with its mathematical meaning in 1655, in his De Sectionibus Conicis, but his choice of symbol is believed to have its origins much earlier, including the Roman numeral for 1,000, which was used to mean many, and consisted of a C, a vertical line, and a backward C to make an image not too dissimilar to mathematical infinity."

Tom drew the symbol on a piece of paper – *CIƆ*

The similarities to that of infinity were instantly recognizable. He said, "But this goes back even further?"

"Yeah, this is based on the ouroboros."

"An ouroboros?" Tom asked.

"It's an ancient symbol depicting a serpent – or in some cases, a dragon – eating its own tail. Originating in ancient Egyptian iconography, the ouroboros entered western tradition via Greek magical tradition and was adopted as a symbol in Gnosticism and Hermeticism and most notably in alchemy."

"What does it mean?"

"The ouroboros is often interpreted as a symbol for eternal cyclic renewal or a cycle of life, death, and rebirth. The skin-sloughing process of snakes symbolizes the transmigration of souls, the snake biting its own tail is a fertility symbol. The tail of the snake is a phallic symbol, the mouth is a yonic or womb-like symbol."

"Really?" Tom asked, wondering for an instant how much she was making up.

"Hey, I'm just passing along what I know." Billie spoke like a university lecturer. "The first known appearance of the ouroboros motif is in the Enigmatic Book of the Netherworld, an ancient Egyptian funerary text in KV62, the tomb of Tutankhamun, in the 14th century BC. The text concerns the actions of the god Ra and his union with Osiris in the underworld. The ouroboros is depicted twice on the figure: holding their tails in their mouths, one encircling the head and upper chest, the other surrounding the feet of a large figure, which may represent the unified Ra-Osiris."

"The Ra-Osiris?" Tom asked.

"Yeah, it refers to Osiris being born again as Ra. Both serpents are manifestations of the deity Mehen, who in other funerary texts protects Ra in his underworld journey. The whole divine figure represents the beginning and the end of time."

Tom said, "All right, so this bronze medallion most likely comes from ancient Egypt?"

"Probably. But there's something else you should know."

"What?"

"The medallion isn't made out of bronze."

"It isn't?"

"No." Billie's tone inflicted upward. "That's orichalcum."

"Orichalcum!" Tom said, thinking about how the dull metal flashed red and gold under the faintest of light. "As in, from the lost city of Atlantis?"

"Exactly!"

"What the hell does that even mean? I thought you said it was Egyptian?"

"It means that that medallion is much older than you first thought."

Tom said, "This all has something to do with the Master Builders then?"

"Almost certainly," she confirmed.

Tom sighed. "I don't suppose you want to hazard a guess about what an ancient artifact, built by the Master Builders of Atlantis have to do with stolen World War II era shipwrecks?"

She laughed. "Not a single clue. But if ever there was someone who could put those two problems together, it's Sam Reilly."

That made Tom think about Sam for the hundredth time since he'd gotten up. "All right, let me know if you can think of anything else."

"I will," she promised. "I'm here if you need me, anytime. Anyplace. Really. I mean it. Where are you going to be?"

Tom's voice hardened. "At *Chelsea and Westminster Hospital ICU*. Waiting for Sam to wake up."

Chapter Thirteen

Tom Bower was good at most everything he did, but one thing he struggled with was waiting, knowing that he was powerless to help in anyway.

He paced in the waiting room throughout the day. When people got irritated by him, he eventually went for a short walk, before returning to wait some more.

A little over 3 p.m. he received a phone call.

The caller ID showed that it was neither Elise or the hospital.

He hit the answer button. "Hello?"

"Tom," the man said, his voice suppressed, like he was waiting to tell him something. "It's James Hunter."

"Hi James, did you find something?"

"Yeah. I messaged some buddies of mine that list of eight shipwrecks. Now the *HMAS Perth* had been slowly stripped over years, but the bulk of its hull was removed in one go in the past couple of days."

"That's right, I remember you telling me."

"Right, that leaves the other seven from the list mostly still intact." James paused, took a breath. "Except, my friends tell me the *USS Houston* just disappeared."

Tom's lips curled into a wry grin. "The whole ship?"

"The whole damned ship in one go. It was completely intact two days ago. Somewhere, in the cloak of darkness, someone has come and salvaged the entire thing. I've never seen anything like it before. Not to this extent. I mean, the *USS Houston* was a Northampton-Class Heavy Cruiser, with a displacement of 9,200 tons. It wasn't cut to pieces by divers, operating like scavengers carving its steel plating bit by bit. Something came along and lifted the entire ship, leaving nothing but a thirty-foot indent in the seabed where the majestic ship's hull once lay."

"How the hell could they do that?"

"Beats me. But I can tell you one thing."

"What?"

"These aren't some opportunistic pirates looking to make money on pre-bomb steel sales. Whoever they are, they're well-funded and they must have a big customer looking for a very specific product."

Tom swore. "That's it!"

"What's it?"

"The list I sent you. It's a shopping list! Someone's trying to buy all eight of those ships. We have to stop them!"

James laughed. "Hey, I agree with you. I have to tell you something, I've spent the last six years working with the Indonesian government trying to keep these illegal salvagers away. It's almost impossible. If they're using a crane large enough to extract an entire ship, then we're going to have trouble stopping it. Besides, if they did that to the *USS Houston* in a night, they'll finish with that shopping list by the end of the week, maybe a fortnight if we include the time it's going to take them to transport to a junkyard."

Tom said, "You're right. I've got to go."

"Where?"

"To stop pirates from stealing the gravesites of World War II naval heroes."

James said, "Good luck."

Tom ended the call and immediately pressed the number for the bridge of the *Tahila*. The phone rang several times before Matthew, the ship's skipper answered.

Tom said, "Matthew, I need you to move the *Tahila* to the Java Sea at full speed. How long will it take you?"

"We're currently refueling in San Francisco. Best we can do is three days."

"Okay, do it."

"Sure. Want to tell me what this is all about?"

"We need to stop illegal salvagers stealing what remains of eight World War II shipwrecks."

Matthew's voice was matter-of-fact. "Obviously. Okay, I'll have the *Tahila* there in three days. How's Sam doing?"

Tom was about to answer him that nothing much had changed, but he spotted Sam's doctor coming out of the ICU. "I've got to go."

He greeted the doctor with a handshake. "How is he?"

The doctor met his eye and said, "Sam Reilly's awake."

Chapter Fourteen

Sam Reilly opened his eyes.

Tom's hardened face was staring back at him, awash with a mixture of concern and relief in equal proportions.

Tom asked, "How do you feel?"

Sam grinned. "Never better..."

"Really?"

"No, I've been shot and my gut hurts like hell!"

A grin broke free across Tom's lips. "The doctor says you'll live."

"Good. I'm not sure if we're going to make that cave dive in Scotland, though..."

"No," Tom agreed. "I spoke to the doctor last night and he said your adventure days will be shut down for a little while yet."

"Forget about what the doctor thinks," Sam said, his habitual insouciance returning. "There are important things to be done."

Tom frowned. "Like what? You just had abdominal surgery. Apparently, the bullet nicked a major vessel. The doctor said something about a mesenteric artery..."

"Sure. He's clamped it or cauterized it or whatever the hell they do with these things. It's as good as new. They also replaced the several bags of blood I appear to have misplaced, thanks to that bullet. So, yeah. I'm good to go. Better, in fact. It's like when you put oil in a car. You're never gonna have more of the stuff than when you first top it up all the way to the line."

"Okay, great. I'll go tell the Doc we're leaving." Tom's dry expression indicated that he felt anything but good about what Sam was saying.

Sam attempted to rise to a sitting position, but agony shot through the muscles in his belly like a lightning strike. He grimaced, swallowed the pain. With Tom's help, he sat up on the bed, looking for his shirt to replace the hospital gown.

Tom smiled, patiently.

Sam had seen that look before. It meant that he thought Sam was acting pig-headed, but that Tom knew him well enough to let him go until he learned his own lesson.

Tom grinned. "So, we're still off to Scotland?"

"Scotland?" Sam frowned. "No, of course not."

Tom let out a deep breath, relief plastered across his face. "Good because you might need to stay in the hospital for a while."

Sam said, "Do you mind finding me some clothes? We need to get going."

"What are you talking about? I thought you'd given up on the idea of going to Scotland?"

"Scotland's out. We don't have time for it. We have somewhere else to be."

"Where?"

Sam looked at him with incredulity. "Where? The Java Sea, Indonesia!"

"But you're injured!" Tom protested.

"Repaired and recovering! There's a difference. Besides, I can rest on board a ship as much as in some London hospital. Even better on the ocean. Fresh sea air! I assume the *Tahila* is on her way?"

Tom's jaw dropped open in a wry expression of confusion. "How did you know I'd dispatch the *Tahila* to the Java Sea?"

Sam said, "Because that's the only way we're going to keep salvagers stealing what remains of eight pre-atomic age shipwrecks."

"Obviously." Tom offered Sam some clothes from the hospital's hand-me downs.

"Is Elise there yet?" he asked, carefully putting an arm into a button-down shirt.

"Elise?" Tom shook his head. "I haven't been able to get in contact with her."

"Missing?"

"Yeah, last anyone heard of her was a week ago when Ben Gellie turned up and said that their parents were still alive, and taking refuge in Shangri-La."

"Of course, she went looking for Shangri-La!" Sam said, memories coming back in jarring flashes. "Now she's missing?"

"That's where we're at. I contacted your global private detective. That guy that you really trust, Steve Cashier. He said his people were able to track her movements down to Jodhpur, India."

"India!" Sam said, buttoning his shirt. "What the hell was she doing there?"

"Steve doesn't know. Apparently, she and Ben took a private nighttime tour of Mehrangarh Fort, before returning to their hotel."

"Then where did they go?"

"He doesn't know. That's where all evidence of their existence dried up." Tom swallowed. "There's one other thing you should know."

"What's that?"

"When the hotel manager noticed that they hadn't checked out of their room, he went upstairs and unlocked their door. Inside he found some fellow wearing a red turban. The man was dead. Murdered. His throat cut."

Sam nodded, taking it all in. He sat on the edge of the hospital bed and tried to pull up his long pants. "Elise will be fine. She can take care of herself. I'm more worried about what we're going to do about the Xianggelila project without her."

Tom asked, "What's the Xianggelila project?"

Sam paused, meeting his eye. "Oh, that's right. You haven't spoken to Elise, so you probably didn't understand much about what was on the USB stick."

"Yeah, not much."

"At least you worked out that timing was everything and that we needed to send the *Tahila* to the Java Sea..." Sam stopped. "Wait, how did you work out...?" Shaking his head, he dismissed the thought midsentence as though the explanation was self-evident.

Tom waited patiently for Sam to finish.

"Don't worry about it. I gather you looked at the list of World War II shipwrecks. This led you to speak to my old friend, James Hunter, who told you all about pre-atomic bomb steel? James would've then investigated the eight wrecks on salvager's shopping lists, then noticed one or two of them have suddenly disappeared. Am I right?"

Tom nodded. A half-grin forming on his parted lips. "Yeah, that's surprisingly pretty accurate, really."

"Good. We need to get going before someone gets the rest of those ships!"

"Wait." Tom said, "What is this all about?"

Sam explained, "Elise intercepted a coded message that someone in China was trying to build a specialized antenna designed to locate Shangri-La."

"Okay, but why is all this a matter of life and death?"

"Because Shangri-La is more than a sanctuary. It's a balancing point on Earth. A place where the puppet-masters reside. Without it, confusion reigns and the world falls into chaos. Yet there's been a disruption in the natural order. A secret organization has held control over Shangri-La for millennia. And right now, people are fighting to reach it, to end that power."

Tom nodded, trying to keep up. "And let me guess. To build this highly sensitive antenna designed to locate Shangri-La, they need unadulterated metals. Iron, copper, bronze and so on, all untouched by nuclear radiation to do it."

Sam grinned, standing up for the first time. "And that's why we need to beat them to it!"

Chapter Fifteen

Strombolicchio Island, Italy

The little wooden fishing boat was painted in a vibrant array of greens, blues, reds and yellows, much like so many others within the Italian fishing community. Its skipper made small inputs into the controls, adeptly maneuvering the vessel closer until its bow nudged the base of the rocky outcrop in the calm waters of the Tyrrhenian Sea.

Elise glanced up at the massive vertical cliffs in awe.

Strombolicchio formed a dark silhouette against the backdrop of the setting sun. Like their fishing boat, the sky was also set in a bruised mixture of yellows, reds, and purple. The volcanic island was famous in the Aeolian Archipelago, a minuscule rock in the sea off the Sicilian coast. The ancient tower of solid lava rose nearly a hundred-and-sixty feet out of the water. Its basalt structure once forming a giant bottle top known as a volcanic plug, formed when magma from a long forgotten volcanic eruption vented out of the sea.

Elise and Ben thanked the skipper and assured him that they didn't need him to wait. They stepped across the gap between the bow and the small landing platform etched into the basalt cliff.

Over the course of the next twenty minutes they clambered up the two-hundred something near vertical stairs, which slowly meandered around the cliff until it reached the level ground at the top of the ancient sea stack.

Elise looked back at the fishing boat, already motoring away.

Her gaze turned toward the lighthouse. A powerful beacon of light shot out of the tower in a series of equally timed bursts. The bright beam erupted in a 360-degree arc for miles.

They walked toward the entrance and stopped.

Elise ran her eyes across the ground, searching for a stone or something to use to break the padlock. Ben ignored her. Walking up to the lock, he removed a key from his pocket, and unlocked the door. He opened the door and spread his hand outward, a gentleman gesturing her to go first.

She suppressed a smile. "You already had the locks changed?"

Ben nodded. "Years ago."

Elise switched on her flashlight and entered the lighthouse.

She didn't climb the circular staircase to the top of the 27-foot tower. Instead, she and Ben descended into a dungeon like stairwell that leveled out into a small opening. The area had once been the living quarters of the lighthouse keeper in years long since passed. The room looked like an anachronism from the 1940s. It was covered in homely green and orange wallpaper of the era. There was a small kitchenette, a single bed, and a short-wave radio. It payed tribute to the time when the keeper doubled up as a radioman and early watchman who kept eyes on various navies as they travelled the area during World War II.

Elise ran her eyes along the walls. There were no windows and no sign of any doors or even any cracks which might suggest a hidden opening.

She turned to Ben. "Do you know where the entrance is?"

Ben nodded. With a smile, he drew another key out of his pocket.

She licked her lips, waited, and watched, as Ben carefully rolled up the Italian rug that covered the middle of the room.

A small trapdoor in the stone tiled floor was barely perceptible. If she hadn't been looking for it specifically, she would have missed it entirely.

Ben removed the copper key and inserted it into a small crease between two stone tiles. He twisted the key, and something gave way with a slight 'clanking' sound.

The tiles, no longer held together by inward force, came away easily.

Ben picked up each of the pieces, carefully placing them to the side of the room, before removing the wooden framework on which they had been placed.

Elise shone her flashlight down the open shaft. Her lips curled into a wry grin. "That's the secret passageway?"

"That's it."

"The one our ancestors, the ancient Master Builders, and most advanced people of the time, constructed?"

Ben nodded. "This is it. Why? What's wrong with it?"

Elise grinned. "It looks more like an oubliette."

Ben shrugged. "It might very well have been used as a dungeon with access only through a trapdoor in its ceiling at some stage. If so, it would've been a very long time ago."

"All right, let's go."

Elise went first, heading down the steep stairwell. She was followed by Ben, who took the time to seal the trapdoor shut behind them.

The passage descended hundreds of feet until Elise felt certain they were well beneath the surface of the Tyrrhenian Sea.

The beams of their flashlights danced across the stairwell before finally opening up into a large cavern. Elise noticed the sounds of their footsteps echoing on the stairs became longer and more distant.

The stairwell finally levelled out.

She shifted the beam of her flashlight around in large swaths, taking in their new surroundings. It was a large cavern, overlooking a passageway that reminded her more of the platform of an underground subway in New York, than of an ancient dungeon beneath a Sea Stack.

The flashlight reflected against water that lined a tunnel made of obsidian – the remnants of the original lava tube. A three-person rowboat made of brass, was tied to a single cleat at the edge of the water.

Elise met Ben's gaze. "I thought we were below sea level?"

"We are."

"Then why doesn't that water rise up and flood this entire area?"

"Because it's not seawater. That's fresh water, most likely rainwater runoff, built up over thousands of years."

She considered that. It made sense. Or at least enough sense that she was willing to keep going. "Now where?"

"We take the boat. The entrance is at the end of this tunnel."

They climbed onto the small rowboat. It wobbled under their weight. Elise shifted her position as low as she could and the little vessel stabilized. There was just one set of oars, and Ben took them. Elise untied the painter, folding it neatly onto the rowboat.

Ben started to row.

The little vessel made its way deeper into the dark tunnel.

At the very end, they reached what appeared to be a dead end.

Elise's purple eyes were wide with wonder. "This is Shangri-La?"

"Not here," Ben informed her.

He swept the wall with the light of his flashlight, searching. The beam stretched from the water all the way up to the ceiling, and across the room, before finally landing on an ended groove in the wall.

Elise grinned.

It was the precise shape of the medallion. Pleased, she removed the ancient artifact from around her neck, then inserted it into the obsidian depression. A moment later, the orichalcum began to glow, turning a golden red.

Behind them, the gateway to Shangri-La opened.

Chapter Sixteen

Java Sea, Indonesia

The black Eurocopter AS350 banked to the north, leaving Jakarta behind as its rotor blades whipped the clear waters of the Java Sea into a frenzy with its thunderous downdraft. The rising sun glistened through the interspaced cloud cover as the helicopter flew at its maximum cruising speed until a ship was spotted in the distance. Its dark, sharp-angled and low-lying hull gave the ship a predator like image, as though it was stalking some sort of mythical quarry beneath the sea.

Along its portside were displayed the words, *TAHILA*

The motor-yacht formed a dark silhouette along the clear, tropical waters. At a length of 180 feet and a beam of 45 feet, it was shaped for speed instead of the comfort of a traditional yacht, with a long black hull and narrow beam tapering into a razor-sharp prow. The trailing whitewash, a stark contrast against the near-black hull against the night's sky, was the only demonstration of the vessel's unique combination of raw power.

She was powered by twin Rolls Royce 28,000hp MTU diesel engines, and twin ZF gearboxes that projected the force of the combined 56,000 hp into four HT1000 HiltonJet waterjets. This power was married to her unique hull, which used a series of hydraulic actuators to alter her shape in order to achieve the greatest speed and stability given any type of sea conditions. *Tahila* was able to lift out of the water onto the aquaplane at speeds of 60 knots – making her the fastest motor yacht of her size in the world.

Sam Reilly grinned with proprietary pride as he laid eyes on her. Everything he held dear in the world was on that ship.

At the helicopter controls, Genevieve signaled that she was about to bring them down. Sam and Tom nodded. She made a quick reconnaissance circle overhead, before quickly placing the Eurocopter's landing skids on the *Tahila's* helipad.

Sam and Tom clambered out onto the ship's sleek deck, while Genevieve finished shutting down the helicopter's systems. The morning sun broke through the clouds, Sam could feel its radiant heat warming his back. He lifted his duffel bag, making a slight grimace as the sudden movement pulled at some of his internal stiches.

Matthew and Veyron were waiting for him on the deck.

Veyron couldn't suppress a big burly grin. "I see you're still making friends wherever you go."

Sam shook his hand with a rueful smile. "I'll be fine."

Matthew's face was set with more genuine concern. "How are you?"

"Really, I'm okay." Sam met his eye with a defiant nod. "Let's go downstairs. Bring me up to speed about how you're going to catch these illegal salvagers."

"Agreed," Matthew replied, heading down the internal stairwell.

Behind them, Genevieve pressed the remote, and the Eurocopter began its descent, silently disappearing into the *Tahila's* storage hold, removing any appearance of its existence. All five of them descended into the heart of the ship.

Sam and Tom dropped their respective duffel bags off into their quarters, before meeting back at the Mission Room a couple minutes later.

Inside the Mission Room, Tom, Veyron, Matthew, and Genevieve sat at the Round Table – a digital masterpiece that was capable of providing 3D holographic renditions of an array of information from building or ship schematics, through to topographic maps.

Lying on the cool deck beside the Round Table, a golden retriever stirred from its near permanent state of dozing. Its ears perked and its tail began to thud the floor in greeting.

Sam grinned. "Hello, Caliburn!"

The dog rolled onto its paws, standing upright. It gave a single, baritone bark of pleasure, but didn't make a bid to greet him.

Sam asked, "What is it?"

Caliburn's head tilted, his doe eyes, a mixture of joy and gentle reproach for leaving him, stared adoringly at him.

Sam kneeled down to scratch Caliburn's mane. The dog immediately forgave him. Trading reproof for uninhibited joy, he nuzzled into Sam's arms.

Sam grinned. "Yeah, I missed you too."

He took a seat at the Round Table and said, "All right, let's hear it… where are we at with these shipwreck thieves?"

Chapter Seventeen

Sam listened as Matthew brought him up to speed.

The *Tahila* had been engaged in a complex game of cat and mouse with multiple salvage operations. By the time they had reached the Java Sea, the *HMAS Perth, Hr. M.s 0-16,* and *HMS Repulse* had been stolen, leaving almost nothing but an indented seabed in their wake.

The illegal salvagers were using two large salvage vessels equipped with magnetic grapples to fish for steel, after divers used a series of detonations to break up the sunken wrecks into smaller, more manageable, pieces. A small armada of barges then transported the steel to an offshore junkyard which was positioned in international waters. These were open areas where no one enforced maritime laws. There the metals were sorted and eventually shipped to China for processing.

When Matthew finished debriefing, Sam said, "I thought they were removing these ships in a single night?"

Matthew nodded. "That's the intel the Indonesian maritime authority provided."

Sam's eyebrows hiked up into a puzzled arch. "But surely there's no way anyone's going to remove any of those huge ships in a single night by simply using explosives, grappling magnets, and an armada of barges."

Matthew turned the palms of his hands upward. "I don't know what to tell you. That's all we've seen so far. Those three vessels were taken before we got here and since we've arrived, no one has made a play for any of the other five shipwrecks."

"Are you certain?"

"Yeah, pretty sure."

Matthew brought up a map of the region on the Round Table. It depicted the Java Sea, an extensive shallow sea on the Sunda Shelf. Lying between the Indonesian islands of Borneo to the north, Java to the south, Sumatra to the west, and Sulawesi to the east. To the north, the Karimata Strait linked it to the South China Sea.

The locations of the five remaining ships were clearly marked, along with their size and depth. Matthew used his fingers to draw another layer into the mapping system. This one showed the real-time GPS locations of each of the known salvage operations, more than a dozen barges, and two junkyards based in international water. There were also another fifteen fishing vessels, which they believed were being used to transport SCUBA divers to the various shipwreck locations.

Matthew turned to Sam and said, "It's now your show, Sam. What do you want to do?"

Sam thanked him and brought up a digital list of the eight World War II era vessels known to be on the salvager's shopping list. He then placed an asterisk next to each of the three sunken ships that had already been taken.

HMAS Perth – Australian Modified Leander Class Battleship.

Hr. M.s 0-16 – Dutch Submarine

USS Houston – United States of America Heavy Cruiser.

HMS Repulse – British Battlecruiser.

HMS Prince of Wales – British Battleship

Chosa Maru – Japanese gunboat.

Sagiri – Japanese Destroyer.

HMS Exeter – British Heavy Cruiser.

"All right, here's our scoreboard, everyone," Sam said, pointing specifically to the three asterisks that indicated the stolen vessels. "Right now, they're winning. Three ships down, five to go. The question is, what sort of game do we want to play?"

Matthew said, "There's not much more we can do. It's all an old-fashioned cat and mouse type game."

"Maybe," Sam said. "Who has another idea?"

Tom licked his lips, smiled. "What if we go on the offensive?"

Sam said, "That could work. What did you have in mind?"

Tom swiped up along the digital table, to bring up the technical data for the three missing shipwrecks. "We know the layout, metallurgy, and basic schematics of the *HMAS Perth, Hr. M.s 0-16,* and *HMS Repulse?*"

Matthew nodded. "Right."

Tom persisted with his line of thinking. "And we know the junkyard where they're being stored and processed is here, just north of the Indonesian island of Bawean."

A half-grin creased Sam's lip. "What are you thinking, Tom?"

Tom smiled. "I'm thinking, why don't we have a sneak peek at that junkyard?"

Matthew asked, "Why? It's in international waters. We can't legally board it, anyway. Even if we did, it wouldn't help us prosecute them."

"That's right," Tom admitted, "But it's also illegal to loot World War II shipwrecks, disturbing the gravesites of thousands of international sailors. Instead of waiting to see who's going to steal the next one, let's get there first."

Sam said, "We confirm the *HMAS Perth, Hr. M.s 0-16,* and *HMS Repulse* are in fact on that junkyard, and then we find out where they're being taken. From there, we'll find out who's searching for Shangri-La."

Matthew said, "You two are crazy!"

Sam shrugged. "Yeah, but I think it beats waiting around here for them to make their next move."

Chapter Eighteen

The dive room at the bottom deck of the *Tahila* housed a unique array of SCUBA equipment, sea scooters, a pair of deep-water Exo-Suits, and a custom designed submersible. All of which could covertly exit the vessel through a purpose built lock out trunk. This way, they could be used in any weather without detection by those on the surface.

Veyron watched over the equipment, his graying beard giving him an air of maturity that the rest of the crew gravely lacked. This was his domain, and he looked after all of the machines with patriarchal love and respect. To the crew, he was more than an engineer. Veyron was a magician with nearly mythical powers who kept the dive equipment operating. They all trusted him with their lives.

Sam Reilly began to don his wet suit.

Tom stared at him through an arched eyebrow. "Really?"

"What?" Sam asked, adjusting his dive gear.

Caliburn gave a loud baritone bark, leveling a reproachful gaze on Sam. His habitually wagging tail remained deadly still.

Sam held up both palms, moving them up and down in a "It's okay, it's okay" manner.

Tom shook his head. "Oh, for goodness sakes, Sam! Even Caliburn knows it's wrong to go SCUBA diving less than a week after major surgery!"

A wry smile ghosted Sam's face. "It'll be a week tomorrow, and it wasn't major surgery... I just lost a lot of blood, that's all." He shrugged. "The doctor said he'd cauterized the artery. So long as it doesn't get nicked by anymore stray bullets, it should be fine."

"Did you mention to him that you intended to go diving?"

"Hey, we're going in by stealth, so we won't even reach thirty feet," Sam said, defending himself. "That's less than one atmosphere. Nothing that's going to cause any stitches to come undone."

"I'm pretty certain you should avoid diving for at least a month after surgery," Veyron gave his advice, his mature face set with casual indifference. If Sam wanted to risk his life, it was neither here nor there to him.

Sam zipped up his wetsuit and Genevieve handed him and Tom a Heckler & Koch MP5, with two additional magazines, each with 30 rounds.

Sam took the weapon, smiled, and asked, "Ah, Genevieve, I knew that you of all people would understand and wouldn't ask me to reconsider. You don't think I'm stupid, do you?"

She made a half-shrug. "Oh, you're being stupid and pigheaded about this Sam, that's for sure. But who am I to argue with you? Besides, maybe the doctors have it wrong?"

Sam nodded. "See, I'm glad you're taking my side."

Genevieve's mouth opened; she stuck her tongue out between parted lips. Then she flashed him an impish and mischievous grin. "After all," she said, "by my reckoning, this is the third time now that you've gone off SCUBA diving after being shot. If it was going to kill you, I suppose it would have happened by now."

"See, I'll be fine."

His jaw set with determination; Tom scanned his equipment. "Okay, let's do this."

Sam reciprocated the buddy check. "Good to go."

He placed his full faced dive mask onto his face, gripped the sea scooter and slowly descended into the partially water filled lockout chamber. Tom followed next to him. When they were ready, Sam pulled the lever and the top of the chamber closed. Once they were sealed inside, incoming ducts opened up, and fresh seawater flowed freely.

When the pressure equalized, the red light on the downward facing door turned to green. The lockout trunk opened.

Sam set a course for the junkyard base and gently powered up the sea scooter's throttle. Its electric motor whined and its propeller whirred.

Then Sam and Tom were on their way to break international laws and investigate what was really going on at the floating steel junkyard.

Chapter Nineteen

The steel junkyard formed a floating island above.

It was built on the largest barge Sam had ever seen. Not just one barge, but four. Each one joined by a series of iron rings that allowed its shape to flexibly shift with the natural movement of the sea. Two tugboats were tied to either end of the barge to ensure the floating island remained within the safety of international waters.

The junkyard cast a dark and ominous shadow, confirming to Sam that they had reached their destination. Sam gently eased the sea scooter next to the barge. Keeping their scooters in a state of negative buoyancy, he and Tom tied them off to a ladder bolted to the barge, where they acted like invisible anchors, waiting for their return.

They removed their diving buoyancy control device, tank, and weight belts, leaving them attached to the sea scooters for their return. Lastly, Sam removed his dive mask and released his grip on the scooter, slowly allowing himself to surface and come alongside the barge.

He wiped the seawater off his face, and took in their new environment at a glance. The side of the barge was protected with a sixty-foot-high steel wall. The wall was broken by a large gap some forty feet to the west of them, where a ship could dock and new cargo was most likely brought on and off the island. There was no sign of anyone at the top of the wall of steel, and no outer railing or platform to suggest that anyone even maintained a security patrol on the floating island.

He expected a crew of people would be living on the junkyard. After all, there would be laborers who sorted the steel from the more valuable fixtures made of brass, copper, or lead. Sam didn't expect the workers themselves would give them much trouble. Yet he also had no doubt that some of the work force on the platform would be equipped with weapons – if only to protect their loot from other pirates.

Sam met Tom's eye. "You ready?"

Tom gave a curt nod. "I'll go first. Make sure it's all right before you come up. The doctor did say to avoid bullets to your stomach for some time."

Sam opened his mouth to argue that he felt fine, just a bit tender, but thought better of it. With a little bow, he gestured outward, and said, "After you."

He watched Tom climb the iron ladder. Despite his size, Tom moved quickly and with the silence of a professional soldier. He paused at the top, glanced across the opposite side, before disappearing inside.

Sam waited for a few seconds, and then followed.

The stitches in his abdominal muscles pulled as he climbed the ladder. He made a slight grimace. He reassured himself the pain was more of a discomfort, and natural given his surgery. Resolute in his decision to be part of the mission, he continued to climb.

At the top of the ladder, he was able to take in the junkyard island in its entirety. Despite climbing sixty feet up the wall of steel that formed the outer hull, the piles of metal scraps continued to rise another fifty feet, forming a small mountain of steel debris at the center, with a small split in the middle, which formed a valley – presumably through which the metals could be moved.

His eyes swept the valley of wreckages. At the far end, roughly half a mile away, a dilapidated crane operated, sifting and sorting large chunks of metal. One person operated the machine from its vantage point some thirty feet in the air. Sam's eyes drifted to the south, where the old officer's quarters of a battleship – still mostly intact – had been wedged beneath the mountain of steel, providing a makeshift living quarters for the crew and workers of the junkyard.

Parked in the front of it was a green Dodge pickup. It didn't look like scrap metal. Instead, it was most likely used for transport by the crew and workers.

Sam's lips pulled down at the corners as he searched for signs of the crew. He didn't believe the entire junkyard was manned by a single crane operator. It didn't matter. He and Tom were armed. They didn't plan on staying around long enough to find out how many people were on the island.

Sam climbed over the wall, slipping behind the protection of a ten-foot-high pile of brass. The sun was low on the horizon, casting long shadows across the junkyard. But the entire barge radiated ambient heat, held there, Sam assumed, by the metal where it was absorbed throughout the day.

He and Tom exchanged a glance.

Sam asked, "What do you think?"

Tom made a crisp reply. "I think something's wrong."

"What?"

"I don't know. There's no evidence of one of our targeted WWII shipwrecks here."

"Maybe they split them into pieces or used explosives?" Sam suggested, although he didn't believe it for a minute.

Tom shook his head. "The hulls of the *HMAS Perth, Hr. M.s 0-16,* and *HMS Repulse* were all taken in a single night. That meant they were plundered from the seabed as whole, or in the very least, split in two or three parts."

Sam stared at the mountains of metal scraps. They were all shards of steel, much more shredded than he would have expected if the salvagers were removing entire ships in a single go. With the exception of the old officer's quarters, which looked like it had been made into a living space for the island's crew, there wasn't a single large section of any vessel. Instead, everything looked like it had been stripped by hand. They were small pieces, more opportunistic than the workings of a highly planned, well financed, specific raids.

He expelled a breath. "Come on, let's go get some photos and see if we can make an affirmative match with any of the three stolen shipwrecks."

"Agreed."

They walked north, slowly making their way through the various mountains of metal scraps. Every time they found a piece of metal that looked like it might be large enough to identify, Sam took a photo of it with his computer tablet.

The device stored schematic, technical, and visual information of every known shipwreck in the area. It quickly made correlations with known sunken vessels, attempting to identify the origins of each piece of steel. Sam took several shots, surprised by how quickly the computer program identified random chunks of steel, digitally matching them with known vessels lost at sea.

Every single one came back as a World War II era shipwreck – just not one of the three that they were looking for.

They slowly made their way around the outer perimeter until they reached the northern side of the junkyard island.

Sam took another thirty shots, but every single one came back negative.

Tom spotted the concerned look on his face. "What do you think?"

Sam said, "We got it all wrong!"

"These aren't illegal salvagers?"

"No, I mean, I'm sure they are. It's just that this operation isn't highly sophisticated. It seems opportunistic. Sure, they're getting in on the salvaged steel trade. But unlike the people we're looking for who have very specific needs and well-funded means of achieving it – this crowd is running a ramshackle operation. Seeking low hanging fruit, the divers in this operation are stripping anything that can be easily taken off any shipwreck."

Tom frowned. "What does that mean?"

Sam swallowed. "It means we've been tracking the wrong salvagers all this time."

Chapter Twenty

Sam was about to say *let's head home,* when he spotted the flicker of light reflecting off steel in the distance. He paused. The flash sparkled again. The entire junkyard, filled with metal, reflected light, but this was different.

Something about it caught his eye. It was too specific to be accidental.

He exchanged a glance with Tom. The two had been friends since childhood, and worked so well together that it didn't take much for either of them to know where they were going with something. In this case, Tom got the hint with almost telepathic prowess. He took a step back and fixed his eyes on the light.

Sam's face was plastered with his habitual insouciance, but his heart was racing. He wanted to duck down and break into a run. It was the wrong move. Whoever was tracing their movements was still a long way off. They thought they were doing the stalking. That meant that they were ahead, if only just. The problem was, if he and Tom ran now, it would give away the game.

Tom said, "I don't mean to risk upsetting the doctor's orders, but I believe someone has a telescopic scope targeted on your head."

Sam fiercely suppressed a primal need to drop down flat on the deck. He forced a smile on his lips and replied, "Technically, the doctor didn't say anything about refraining from head shots, just abdominal wounds. I don't suppose it's just a telescope, no weapon?"

"Afraid not, there's a long barrel sticking out from under it."

Sam expelled a breath. "All right, that's makes it less likely it's a telescope by itself. Can you see anyone else?"

"No, just the one."

Sam frowned. "That seems unlikely to me. I mean, this entire place, and we have a crane operator and someone with what we must assume is a rifle. It doesn't seem probable."

"Agreed. So the question remains, where are the rest of them?"

They kept walking, trying to find somewhere to disappear. A series of metal objects had been stacked in such a way as to create an artificial tunnel beneath one of the mountains of scrap metal. Sam turned to step inside, instantly feeling better as soon as he knew the rifle scope was no longer tracing him.

He and Tom paused inside their steel passageway. Although, Sam realized, passageway was the wrong word. The place was more like a succession of metallic caves, each one joining together to create a seemingly endless tunnel which descended all the way to the bottom of the valley of steel.

Sam whispered. "What do you think?"

"If we follow this, we'll stay out of the sniper's sight, but we're going to be sitting ducks once we reach the bottom of the valley."

Sam paused, his lips contorted with momentary indecision. "So we're stuck. It's a classic catch 22."

He turned to look at the sound of people coming from behind them.

The junkyard was no longer empty.

It had a small crew of workers, who had formed a not-so-minor militia in the event of an attack. They were all equipped with machine guns. By the looks of things, they weren't there to patrol. They had been rounded up, and were in the process of preparing to attack.

Which meant they had known about Sam and Tom.

Tom was the first one to get it. "There must be a digital proximity alarm!"

"Looks like it," Sam said, his voice hard. "They've known about us since we first arrived. No wonder we couldn't see any crew. They were preparing for a full on assault. They must have been surprised to find just the two of us."

Tom looked at them moving in the distance, trying to cast a net of militia to capture them. "Their response doesn't look any less deadly."

Sam nodded. "Well, that decides it then. We're heading down to the valley."

Chapter Twenty-One

Sam ducked into the iron cave system.

A ripple of machine gun fire followed him, giving him just the right amount of encouragement to keep going despite the strong pains in his gut. He moved with surprising speed and agility for someone a week out of major surgery.

The splintered passageway felt more like a steel canyon, with multiple conjoining caverns, narrow slots, and giant boulders of crushed steel to clamber over. He imagined in the heavy rain of the tropics it would flow like a canyon too.

Following right behind, their attackers moved even faster.

Shots pelted the plate steel, ricocheting effortlessly off the old naval ballistic armor. Sam thanked the old metallurgists, who knew how to build steel to resist bullets. Quickly shuffling across a large chunk of steel, the remnants of an old coal fired boiler, Sam slid down a sixteen-foot drop. He grunted with pain when he reached the ground below.

Tom paused at the top, having a clean shot straight up the tunnelway. He released several rounds upwind – taking out three people – before turning and following Sam down.

At the bottom of the steel canyon, the iron cave opened up into the valley. Sam spotted the living quarters he'd seen when they first climbed onto the barge. It looked empty. His eyes swept the valley of scrap metal. There was a mostly straight road – if you wanted to call it that – which ran the length of the floating junkyard, before opening up to a docking platform used by cargo ships.

If they could reach it, they could get to the water. Sam couldn't see anyone in the living quarters, or nearby. All his attackers appeared to be coming right behind them. He tentatively stepped out into the valley.

A shot rang out.

The ground five feet to his right sparked as a bullet ripped into the steel hull of the barge. Sam dived to the ground, retreating behind more World War II armor plating, as the shooter followed through with several shots.

A second and third shooter, having spotted them, began emptying their rounds down the clear path of the valley.

Sam sat with his back up against the protection of the steel wall and waited. An intermittent barrage of shots came from where they had recently been. Each one seeming to fall closer to them than the ones before, as the militia made their way through the steel canyon, slowly encroaching on their temporary sanctuary.

One of the attackers entered Tom's line of sight, and he released a single shot, hitting the man's upper torso, and knocking him down.

Sam exchanged a meaningful glance with Tom, who was still guarding their rear.

Tom frowned and shook his head. "How do you do it?"

Sam licked his dry lips. "What?"

"You keep coming awfully close to breaking your doctor's orders and getting shot again."

"I know, I know. I'll try to do better next time. Honestly, I didn't think there would be people guarding it with machine guns. It's not like anyone's going to come along and rob them of several thousand tons of steel."

Both men laughed.

It was a stupid joke, given the high possibility that they were both going to die.

Sam stopped laughing, his eyes narrowed, and his jaw became set with determination. "All right, we can't sit here all day. Which way do you want to go Tom?"

Tom grinned, his bravado outstripping obvious fear. "We can head straight up this canyon," he said, pointing the direction. "But it's going to take a while for me to take out the remaining militia."

"Right, that's what I was thinking too." Sam's eyes, darted toward the valley, to the darkness of the open sea at the end. "That water looks so close, doesn't it?"

Tom expelled a breath. "Uh-huh. Looks really easy to get to. If only there was a way to get there without being shot by the people up there with guns trained on us."

"Yeah, that's what I was thinking."

Their attackers from behind were almost upon them. Tom fired a couple well placed shots up range, giving their lethal pursuers pause. "If only there was a way to protect ourselves along that valley."

Sam grinned. "Maybe there is."

Chapter Twenty-Two

The sheet of iron was roughly five feet long and two wide. It weighed more than a hundred pounds and was going to be awkward as hell to carry. The piece looked like it had simply been cut off the side of a hull. Three quarters of a century of rust had thinned the armor plating, making it lighter, but still thick enough to resist anything less than armor penetrating rounds.

Sam said, "Give me a hand. What do you think of our new shield?"

Tom gave it an appraising look at a glance. "It'll do."

Together they pulled the sheet out from a stack of scrap metal. It was hard enough just to slide it, let alone getting it up in the air.

They exchanged a quick look.

It was going to be tough to lift, but it was their only chance of surviving. They couldn't shoot their way out, and one way or another, they were going to need to reach the end of the steel valley.

Tom said, "Count of three?"

Sam gave a curt nod. "Okay, one, two, three..."

Together, they gave a firm heave, pulling the iron sheet up to their chests.

Tom said, "Half way there."

Sam took a deep breath. "Ready?"

"Yeah."

"Okay, lift."

They lifted it up over their heads.

The thing felt like it weighed a ton.

Behind them, two attackers reached the bottom of the steel cavern.

Tom was the first to react. "Sam, let go!"

Sam dropped the iron sheet, while Tom lifted his end up. The armor turned straight upright to form a shield. It wasn't much, but it was enough to protect them from the first set of shots. That was all they needed.

A sharp burst of bullets pinged as they struck the armor.

Sam unslung his MP5 submachine gun. In one single movement, unconsciously working on muscle memory from years of training, he lined up the barrel, and squeezed the trigger. It was set to "F," meaning it was in fully automatic mode.

The shots ripped through their two attackers, killing them both.

Sam removed the empty magazine, replacing it with a full one. "Last one!"

Tom said, "Let's not wait to use it. Let's get out of here."

"Agreed!"

Tom lowered his side of the shield, and Sam picked up the other end. The new surge of adrenaline gave him the last bit of strength needed to lift the iron over their heads. Sam breathed heavily under the strain, while Tom looked like he could probably carry it all day.

Tom said, "I don't mean to complain, but this is gonna hurt trying to carry this half a mile to the other end of the valley."

Sam huffed. "Don't worry, I've got a better idea."

Tom said, "I'm all ears!"

"See that green Dodge over there?"

"Yeah."

"It's in too good a condition to be used for scrap, which means they drive it."

Tom asked, "How are you planning on getting it started?"

"The keys will be in the ignition. On a floating junkyard, there's no reason to ever take them out. Why bother?"

"What if you're wrong?"

Sam's lips turned into a hard line. "Then we're probably dead."

"All right."

A second later, they started to make their run for the Dodge.

As soon as they were out in the open, bullets rained down upon them bringing a cacophony of pinging sounds, like hard and lethal rain. They moved quickly and huddled beneath their shield. It seemed to hold and protect them, but their safety was anything but a certainty. Anything could happen. They could still trip, or drop the shield, or a stray bullet could ricochet off the steel flooring and get lucky, killing them in the process.

And the shield was heavy.

Sam was struggling.

Tom could tell. It might have been the recent injury, or simply the weight of the shield. Either way, Sam looked like he was in trouble, which meant they were both in trouble. "Are you okay, Sam?"

Sam made a curt nod. "I'll make it. Now I know how Charles D'Albret felt when his men were pummeled by a barrage of arrows fired by English longbows at the Battle of Agincourt."

"Let's hope this ends up better for us than it did for the French army!"

Sam gritted his teeth and pushed on, regretting the analogy, as he remembered that D'Albret died at Agincourt after being pierced by an arrow.

About thirty seconds later they reached the Dodge.

Sam rested his end of the shield on the roof of the pickup, opened the door and climbed in. He quickly shuffled through to the driver's side. Tom slid the remainder of the iron sheet onto the roof and followed Sam inside.

Sam felt for the key.

It was right where he'd hoped it would be – in the ignition.

Sam grinned. "What do you know? Hey, you win some!"

He turned the ignition.

But the Dodge pickup wouldn't start.

Chapter Twenty-Three

Sam tried turning the key again.

The ignition made that clicking sound, but no engine activity. No sound of the pistons trying to turn over.

Tom said, "The battery's dead! The same thing used to happen to my dad's Dodge." He glanced around at the older cabin. "It was probably about the same age as this one, too."

Sam frowned. "That's great. How did he fix it?"

"He used to leave a pair of jumper leads on the back seat."

Sam glanced over his shoulder and swore.

There was a jump starter battery pack on the back seat.

Above them, intermittent pinging sounds on the roof confirmed they were still being shot at. Sam turned to Tom. "So do you want to get out and try, or you want me to have a go?"

"I'll go," Tom said.

Sam raised his eyebrows. "Are you sure?"

"No, but I've done this before on my dad's Dodge. I'll be quicker than you."

"Okay," Sam said, removing his MP5 submachine gun. "I'll provide cover."

Tom grabbed the battery pack and cursed. "Don't bother."

"Why not?"

"The battery pack is dead, too."

By now their pursuers from the steel canyon had reached the deck and were starting to shoot at them. The Dodge was a big pickup, but contrary to what Hollywood might have you believe, the average American motorcar offered little in the way of protection from machine gun fire.

Sam and Tom ducked down.

Bullets peppered the truck, splintering and shattering the front and rear windshield. When the shooting stopped, Tom sat up, pushed what remained of the rear windshield out so that he had a clear line of sight, and began to provide return fire.

Sam tried turning the key again.

It was a long shot, but he needed to get lucky.

He was greeted by the same clicking sound.

Sam paused. "Anything else it could be?"

"No. My dad's Dodge was as reliable as they come. There were only two reasons why the pickup ever failed to start."

"One was a dead battery..." Sam said, "What was the other?"

"He had a kill switch installed."

Sam grinned. "Just out of curiosity, where did he put that?"

Tom glanced at the steering wheel. "On his one, it was just down there on the left under the dash."

Sam reached down and felt the underside of the dash. There was a single metal switch. He flicked it forward.

And tried turning the ignition key.

The 239 cubic inch, 175 hp engine turned over, starting with a gravelly roar. Behind them, machine gun fire began to rake the pickup.

Sam released the handbrake, threw the gear stick into drive, and floored the accelerator. The Dodge jumped forward.

He turned the wheel, bringing them around, and along the steel valley – heading for the loading dock. With one hand, he put his seatbelt on, hearing the familiar click of the buckle.

Sam kept his foot planted and the Dodge kept picking up speed. "You might want to put on your seatbelt. This is going to be a rough landing!"

Tom emptied his last magazine trying to deter their attackers. His eyes darted toward the end of the deck, where Sam was racing toward the water at thirty miles an hour. Quickly feeling for the seatbelt, he clicked it in place.

The Dodge kept picking up speed all the way to the end of the floating junkyard. Following right behind them, their attackers emptied their magazines down range, ripping into the back of the pickup.

The Dodge plowed off the end of the deck and flew through the sky – seemingly suspended in midair. As expected, gravity won out. The vehicle dove downward, and they crashed into the Java Sea.

Sam felt his head jolt forward as the hood hit the water, sending a heavy ocean spray through the missing windshield. Everything was foaming whitewash for a few seconds, as turbid water flooded the cabin.

The Dodge seemed to float for a few seconds. Sam took the chance to take a couple of deep breaths, before the heavy engine began to pull the truck down from the front.

Sam fought to unclip his seatbelt. In a panic, it seemed harder than normal, but it came free in the end. His eyes gave a cursory glance at Tom who was already calmly swimming out through the non-existent rear windshield.

Both their heads bobbed up above water a couple seconds later.

Catching their breath, they surface swam toward their sea scooters. But their attackers hadn't given up yet. Having run the length of the steel valley, someone had reached the dock and spotted them. There were shouts of recognition, and then a new barrage of gunfire.

Sam and Tom didn't wait to see where the bullets landed.

They dipped down, swimming deep, and across.

Their sea scooters were visible in the clear water. It was a long swim, but both of them were excellent free divers. Their lungs burned, but they reached their SCUBA gear without having to surface again.

Sam placed his mask across his face, purged the seawater, and took a joyous breath of cool, sweet, air.

Seconds later, they were on their way back to the *Tahila*.

Chapter Twenty-Four

Inside the *Tahila,* Sam exited the lockout locker, floating up to the surface.

He was met by Matthew, Veyron, and Genevieve. They all wore a decidedly concerned look on their faces, although Genevieve's was mixed with an evident desire to join the fight.

"We heard machine gun fire," Matthew said, his voice hard and cold, his pale blue eyes uneasy.

Sam cut him off with the wave of his hand. "We're fine. They just don't like visitors, that's all."

Genevieve said, "Did you find what you were looking for?"

"No." Sam shook his head. "What's worse, is it looks like we've been wrong about everything. The *HMAS Perth, Hr. M.s 0-16,* and *HMS Repulse* was never on that barge!"

A puzzled look creased Matthew's face. "But we've been tracking the area since we got here. The metals from those vessels couldn't have been taken anywhere else!"

Sam shrugged. "I don't know how they're doing it, but I do know what our next move is."

Matthew asked, "What?"

Sam said, "We need to send divers down to the remaining five shipwrecks."

"Why?" Matthew asked, "We've got satellites fixed on those locations. No one has been there since the *Tahila* reached the Java Sea. There's no way any ships have been there."

"I agree, but they moved the *HMAS Perth, Hr. M.s 0-16,* and *HMS Repulse* somehow without anyone seeing it! And if they can do that, there's no reason to think that they would stop simply because we arrived."

Matthew turned to go. "I'll set a course for the *HMS Exeter* right away. The British Heavy Cruiser is the closest shipwreck on our list. We can be there within the hour."

The *Tahila* could move at 60 knots when it needed to. As far as Sam was concerned, that was right now. Sam showered, changed into dry clothes, and then waited on the bridge.

Five minutes shy of the hour, Matthew said, "We're approaching the wreck site."

"Very good," Sam said, glancing at the map. "Take us right above the *HMS Exeter*. I want to get a good bathymetric reading of the wreckage."

"Understood."

Matthew adjusted the throttles, and, using the small joystick, he maneuvered the *Tahila* into a basic grid-search of the area. Not that there was much searching needed. The *HMS Exeter* had a marker buoy directly above it, for recreational SCUBA divers to use for their descent and ascent.

Sam stared at the bathymetric readout as they searched for the shipwreck. He double checked the GPS location and the identical bathymetric charts for the gravesite. The two matched the current readings exactly.

That's when he swore.

Because, the *HMS Exeter* was missing.

In its place, was a thirty-foot crater that ran a hundred eighty feet long – the shape of a ship's hull in an otherwise flat seabed.

Chapter Twenty-Five

Within twenty-four hours, Sam had confirmed that seven of the eight World War II shipwrecks had been stolen, leaving the *USS Houston* – an American Heavy Cruiser – as the sole surviving vessel. The *Houston* was their last chance of finding out who was responsible for the thefts, and more importantly, who was searching for Shangri-La.

"Hold the *Tahila* here, Matthew," Sam said, standing up. "Tom and I are going for a dive."

Matthew asked, "Why? We already know that sunken wreck is still here. You have bathymetry, there's no reason to go down there just to keep your eyes on it."

"I don't trust it. I'd feel better looking at that wreck with my own eyes."

Matthew gave a half-shrug. "Okay, suit yourself. How long do you plan on staying down there to keep your eyes on the shipwreck?"

Sam matched his grin, but bit back any retort. "Tom and I will place several GPS transducers on the hull. That way, when our would-be thief attempts to steal the ship, we'll be able to keep track of where they take it."

"Right," Matthew acknowledged. "That makes more sense."

Sam and Tom donned their dive gear and were in the water within twenty minutes. It was night time and Sam wasn't going to risk having the last ship stolen right under their noses while they slept.

The *USS Houston* was resting in 90 feet of water. The visibility was poor – roughly three feet – with a lot of natural debris and rust particles blurring their vision. It wasn't a deep dive, but it wasn't shallow either. They were diving on twin air tanks, but would need to be quick about it, because at that depth, they weren't going to get a lot of bottom time.

Sam switched on his flashlight and made the descent quickly, following the guideline tied off to the *USS Houston's* bow used by recreational divers. He swallowed to equalize the pressure in his ears. As they approached the seabed, the heavily encrusted hull of the *USS Houston* came into view.

Swimming closer, Sam reached out and touched the bow to make sure it was real. He smiled and depressed his dive radio mic. "Well Tom, at least she's still here."

"Yeah, that's something."

Sam placed the first GPS transmitter – attaching it magnetically to the hull. "All right, let's keep going."

They placed another five transmitters along the length of the hull.

On their return run, Sam stopped at the entrance to the bridge. The beam of his flashlight lingering on something inside. Its hatchway had long since been removed and recreational divers were obviously using the ship's bridge as a swim through.

Tom met his eye. "What are you doing, Sam?"

"I'm going to go in. I won't be long."

Tom glanced at his dive gauge. They had air left, but it wasn't plentiful. They weren't there on a pleasure dive. He asked, "Why?"

"I want to place one more GPS tracker inside the bridge. Just in case someone decides to start cutting the hull into pieces, I want to make sure we can still track the *USS Houston*. After all, this is our last chance of catching these grave robbers and hopefully finding Shangri-La."

"All right," Tom said. "But let's be quick about it."

"Agreed."

Sam kicked his fins, swimming through the open hatchway. The beam of his flashlight flickered on the narrow passageway. Tom followed him in a few seconds later. Sam searched the area, shining his flashlight across the inside of the inky dark bridge.

He found a place near the helm with a line of sight through the windshield and placed the GPS tracker. If the shipwreck was cut in two, or someone went to the effort of removing the GPS trackers from the hull, this would be their last means of keeping track of the *USS Houston.*

Sam said, "All done, let's head home."

Tom said, "Sounds good."

Sam turned to make his way out of the bridge and stopped, because all of a sudden, the entire *USS Houston* began to move.

Chapter Twenty-Six

On board the bridge of the *Tahila*, Matthew watched the humongous vessel approach. His eyes narrowed as he took it in. The ship was easily 600 feet long, if not more. Three towers dominated its deck, with one giant derrick tower in the middle rising more than a hundred feet into the air, followed by two A-frame towers on either side, giving the ship the appearance of an exploratory oil drilling rig.

The strange ship made a direct approach toward the *USS Houston,* slowing to a complete stop directly above the World War II shipwreck.

Genevieve stared at it. "What the hell is it?"

Matthew shook his head. "It looks like a drilling rig, but there's no reason it would be placing exploratory drilling cores at the same site as the *USS Houston.*"

"Do you think it's some sort of salvage vessel?"

The lines across Matthew's face deepened. "I don't know. It would explain what the vessel's doing here, but the decking's all wrong for a salvage ship."

Genevieve's blue eyes flashed interest. "How so?"

"A salvage vessel might utilize a giant derrick tower to house a crane, but at the end of the day, it needs a large open space on the deck for whatever salvaged pieces to be placed. If you look at this ship here, the entire decking space is filled with cranes, and an intricate system of mechanical pulleys. These were most likely used to raise and lower the incredibly long drilling heads which need to extend all the way down to the seabed."

Genevieve considered that. "You're right. There's nowhere on board to place the *USS Houston* even if they could retrieve it in a single go."

Matthew watched as the ship began to engage part of its drilling rig. Giant cables could be seen running through their intricate system of pulleys extending to the top of the derrick tower, and out in each direction of the deck.

Genevieve suppressed a grin. "Still think they're not stealing the *USS Houston*?"

"I have no idea. Either way, I'm going to contact the Indonesian Maritime Authority. Stealing or not, someone's going to want to know about a drilling rig operating directly above the wreckage of an historic shipwreck."

"Good idea. I'm going to go find Veyron. As an engineer, he might have a better idea what they're trying to do."

Matthew nodded, and dialed the number for their contact in the Indonesian Maritime Authority and briefed him about what was going on.

Twenty minutes later, the ship began to motor away.

Matthew brought up the bathymetric readings of the seabed.

The *USS Houston* was missing.

A puzzled look flashed across Matthew's face. "How the hell did they do that?"

Veyron stepped onto the bridge, glanced at the strange vessel, and said, "My God! That's the *Hughes Glomar*!"

Chapter Twenty-Seven

Genevieve stared at the massive vessel.

Matthew immediately set a course to track it. Sam and Tom were most likely on board the *USS Houston*, which meant they were now on board the *Hughes Glomar*. Irrespective of where they were, the *Tahila* needed to make sure it didn't lose the shipwreck. Sam and Tom could surface any time they wanted and switch their own personal locator beacons on, whereupon Genevieve could take the Eurocopter and retrieve them out of the water.

Veyron said, "I thought she was sold to China and dismantled for scrap metal, but evidently, they decided to keep her, because here she is!"

Genevieve turned to Veyron. "What's the *Hughes Glomar*?"

Veyron's eyes widened with shock, his voice taking on a reflective tone. "The *Hughes Glomar Explorer* was a deep-sea drillship platform built for Project Azorian."

Genevieve asked, "Project Azorian?"

"Yeah, that was the name for the secret 1974 effort by the United States Central Intelligence Agency's Special Activities Division to recover the Soviet submarine *K-129*, which was sunk in the Pacific Ocean, some 1,600 miles northwest of Hawaii."

"You tried to steal one of our nuclear subs?" She feigned concern, but despite being born in Moscow, and growing up in the Soviet Union during the Cold War, she felt little connection to her mother country.

Veyron gave an apologetic nod. "It was the Cold War. The US looked to any edge it could get."

She folded her arms across her chest. "So they built that ship to steal *K-129* from the depths of the Pacific seabed?"

"That's the gist of it."

"How did they keep a project like that secret?" she asked.

"They didn't." Veyron grinned, his eyes distant, as though recalling an interesting story from his childhood. "Famous filmmaker and aviator, Howard Hughes was approached by the CIA to be the face of the project. He told the media that the ship's purpose was to extract manganese nodules from the ocean floor. This marine geology cover story became surprisingly influential, causing many others to examine the idea."

"Did it work?"

"Sort of. The ruse worked. The recovery of *K-129* not so much. In 1974, the *Hughes Glomar* salvaged a portion of *K-129*, but as it was being lifted to the surface, a mechanical failure in the grapple caused two-thirds of the section to break off. This lost segment of the sub was said to have held many of the most-sought items, including the code book and nuclear missiles. The recovered section held two nuclear-tipped torpedoes and some cryptographic machines, along with the bodies of six Soviet submariners. These men were given a formal, filmed burial at sea."

Genevieve asked, "How did the Chinese get hold of a CIA sponsored salvage vessel?"

"It's a long story."

"Go on," she said, her lips parting in an impish smile. "We've still got time before the authorities intercept and board the *Hughes Glomar*."

Veyron nodded. "Okay, give me a second to recall what I know about the ship's sad demise."

"No rush."

"Thanks." Veyron took a seat in a big leather chair opposite the sonar monitors. "After *Project Azorian* ended there was little interest in keeping the vessel going."

"The Navy didn't try to appropriate it for something else?"

"There's very little else it could do." Veyron pursed his lips. "While the ship had an enormous lifting capacity, there was little interest in operating the vessel because of her great cost. From March to June 1976, the General Services Administration published advertisements inviting businesses to submit proposals for leasing the ship."

"Any takers?"

"Seven in total, but none of them amounted to anything. One was from a man who said he planned to seek a government contract to salvage the nuclear reactors of two United States submarines. The Lockheed Missile and Space Company submitted a US$3 million, two-year lease proposal contingent upon the company's ability to secure financing, Lockheed never found the financial backers it needed."

"In the end, what happened?"

"Although the scientific community rallied to the defense of the *Hughes Glomar*, urging the President to maintain the ship as a national asset, no agency or department of the government wanted to assume the maintenance and operating cost. Subsequently, during September 1976, the *Hughes Glomar* was transferred to the Navy for storage and dry docking."

"I can't quite remember all the details, but basically it was eventually leased by a mining company to perform deep sea drilling projects, before being sold off to a Chinese scrap metal yard for salvaging."

Genevieve could picture it now. "Where someone got the idea to use it to salvage World War II era, low nuclear radiation steel and other metals."

"Exactly."

The *Tahila* kept tracking the *Hughes Glomar*. They watched as a small taskforce consisting of the Malaysian Coast Guard and Indonesian Maritime Authority – backed by two small boarding parties from its Navy – homed in on an intercept course.

Genevieve gave a wicked smile as she watched the scene unfold. "This should be interesting."

Matthew's jaw was set firm, concern flashed across his eyes. "I don't know. It all seems too easy."

"What are you talking about?" Genevieve countered. "They managed to salvage seven of the eight ships before anyone caught up with them."

"Exactly. So why are they allowing themselves to be captured now?" Matthew's eyes narrowed. "These aren't amateurs trying to make a quick buck. They're professionals, with a massive budget."

They watched as the boarding crews ordered the *Hughes Glomar* to heave to and prepare to be boarded.

The ship slowed to a stop.

Genevieve's lips lifted in a half-smile. "So good so far."

Matthew's chin dipped in a crisp nod. "I agree. I almost didn't expect them to stop."

Genevieve said, "Maybe Sam and Tom are on board and have already reached the bridge?"

"That's possible. It's the sort of stupid idea Sam would get into his crazy heroic mind. And of course, Tom seeing no argument against it, would go along with the idea."

Genevieve said, "A hundred bucks says the ship heaved to because Sam and Tom made them. Any takers?"

Matthew shook his head. "No way. I know Sam and Tom… they're almost certainly on board by now."

She turned to Veyron. "What about you?"

"Not a chance!" came Veyron's sharp reply. "I'll keep my hundred dollars, thank you. Sam and Tom are on that ship prepared to cause havoc as we speak."

Genevieve gave a snort of laughter, then stared up at the *Hughes Glomar*. Its deck and three giant towers were brightly lit up with powerful spotlights from the Indonesian Maritime Authority's ships.

A second later, the *Hughes Glomar* exploded.

The internal blast ripped through the massive ship's hull, instantly splitting it in two. Each end floundered for a few minutes, before the heavy iron hull slipped under the water. The *Hughes Glomar* vanished, dragged to the seabed three hundred feet below their keel.

Chapter Twenty-Eight

The capture vehicle was fundamentally an oversized steel claw with a series of hydraulic rams, designed to lock into place, and encapsulate the entire wreckage of the *USS Houston*.

Sam Reilly had used a similar system himself, but had never heard of one being built to this scale before. The capture vehicle was then affixed to a large cable, which presumably was attached to a derrick mounted on the deck of a salvage ship.

It took under a minute to seal the gigantic ship the *USS Houston* within its grip. Neither men spoke about the lethal situation they were in. They knew they needed to get out while they still had the chance.

Tom was closer to the exit, so he led the way. Sam kicked his fins hard, moving quickly through the internal passageway trying to keep up. Ahead, the beam of Tom's flashlight flickered across the cold steel gangway and illuminated their path.

Up ahead, Tom's flashlight had become fixed on one point.

Sam stopped kicking, allowing his momentum to carry him slowly to the place where Tom had paused.

Through the radio, he heard Tom's garbled voice. "Sam, we have a problem."

Sam fixed his flashlight where the open hatchway should have been. In its place was the solid steel arm of the capture vehicle.

"Of all the shitty luck... the hydraulic ram had to be wedged into our only exit!"

"Afraid so," Tom confirmed.

"Any way around it?" Sam asked, hopeful.

"Not through here."

Sam checked his dive gauge. There were still 100 bars of air left, so they were in no immediate danger of drowning. They still had time, but it would dwindle quickly if they remained trapped inside the sunken ship. What's more, there was a good chance the salvage vessel would bring the wreckage straight to the surface, preventing them from making a decompression stop along the way.

He had no intention of getting the bends today.

Sam reached into a zipped pouch on the side of his buoyancy control device and extracted his computer tablet. It stored the schematics of the *USS Houston* along with current recreational diving notes for the wreck site.

He scrolled through the dive notes.

There were four entry and exit points still accessible on the *USS Houston.* Two at the aft gun bay. One at the forward hatch, and just one connected to the bridge.

Sam's heart pounded in his chest.

They were trapped.

He was about to close the diving reference material, but a warning note caught his attention. He clicked on the alert:

The USS Houston has three potential entry points that should never be used. These are located on the port side, amidships on E-deck, and two at the stern. These were created by torpedo shots during the ship's original sinking. The blast marks have resulted in razor sharp shrapnel scars in the hull, making a deadly navigational hazard for divers, and should be avoided at all costs.

A bubble of elation rippled through Sam as he realized a solution.

He brought up the *USS Houston* schematics.

Tom fixed his flashlight on the computer tablet. The closest breach in the hull was the one amidships on E-deck. It was six decks below the bridge. Sam ran his eyes along the series of descending ladders, passageways, and rooms that stood between them and the outside world. It was like trailing your finger along one of those mazes they have for children.

Only in this case, if they made a wrong turn, they would drown.

Sam began running through the intricate route again. One mistake and they would not have enough air to backpedal.

Tom said, "I can get us there."

Sam knew that Tom was probably the best cave diver in the world. His mind worked like a computer in seemingly impossible caves. On paper, the route looked easy enough, but the fact was, trying to navigate in the isolated darkness inside a shipwreck with near zero visibility was next to impossible.

"All right, I'll be right behind you."

Tom brought his knees to his chest, and using his hands to pull himself through, he turned around in the tight confinement of the steel passageway, heading back toward the bridge. Once Tom was past him, Sam turned around, and began to follow.

In the darkness of narrow passageways that turned in every direction, and each one appearing nearly identical, it was easy to become disoriented. To make matters worse, by artificially maintaining neutral buoyancy, it was easy to lose track of which way was up or down.

Mentally cross-referencing his location inside the *USS Houston*, Tom slowed at the end of the passageway. He shone the beam of his flashlight in a concentrated arc from left to right, before settling on a dark patch below.

A few seconds later, Sam watched Tom disappear down the internal stairwell. He waited until his friend had reached the bottom and was making his way across to the next section, before beginning his own descent.

Sam kept his computer tablet open to the ship's schematics, so that he could trace his movements with his finger. Commencing from the known location of the bridge, he was able to maintain his situational awareness despite having little or no frame of reference as he continued deeper into the bowels of the World War II wreck.

The stairwell was really a near vertical ladder-well. Sam had to swallow to equalize his ears as he made the sharp descent.

There were four ladder-wells to navigate.

Sam reached the bottom one. Pursuing Tom's light, he turned left, before making a dog-leg through a series of narrow passageways. An exit to the open sea should be up ahead. Unfortunately, the passageway had buckled and warped over time. As a result, it was quite narrow at this section.

Up ahead, Tom swore.

Sam asked, "What is it?"

Tom said, "The torpedo must have ripped through this section, bending the steel inward. We can't get through this way."

Chapter Twenty-Nine

Sam ran his eyes across the schematics on his tablet.

He pressed his mic and said, "Tom, there's another way through. If we head down another level, we can come up again on the other side of this thing."

Tom replied, "Okay. Your turn to lead."

Sam spun around and began kicking his fins in slow, purposeful movements. In his left hand he kept the tablet open, making sure that he didn't make a navigational mistake, and in his right hand, he held a flashlight. The beam wisped through the silt beads which had been already stirred from their recent movement through the passageway.

He reached the descending ladder-well and immediately dropped down it, diving head first. At the bottom he was greeted by an Indonesian Catshark. The creature was roughly four feet long, its green eyes stared right at him.

Sam continued swimming, and the small species of ground shark turned to swim away. It was a good sign. The Catshark wasn't big, but it wasn't small either. It was unlikely to want to wander too far from natural sunlight. That meant they were close to the exit.

He checked his map, swam across the gangway, down a small set of stairs, before swimming up through a vertical ladder.

Sam expelled a breath of air as he began to ascend. His head popped up through the hatchway. He swept the new room with the beam of his flashlight. It was virtually demolished, with several bulkhead walls bent inward, as though part of the ship had imploded as it sank.

They were in the right place.

He turned around, and the light vanished into a dark void.

Sam grinned. "It worked, Tom. We've found a way out!"

"That's great!" Tom replied, "Because I'm just about out of air!"

They slipped through the lethal shards of fractured steel and swam out into the open sea. As soon as they were free from the *USS Houston*, they could see how the illegal salvagers had been getting away with stealing the World War II wrecks for so long.

The capture vehicle, which encapsulated the shipwreck, was being transferred from the cable system off a salvage ship, across to a purpose-built transporter submarine. Presumably, the surface ship would appear like a drilling rig, going from place to place without ever removing a wreck out of the water.

Sam would have liked to stay and see where the submarine went, but without glancing at his dive gauge, he knew they wouldn't have the air supply to make it. Besides, they didn't have any weapons with them, so there was nothing they could do once they got there.

He watched the submarine go, taking with it the *USS Houston* and the remains of the final eight World War II shipwrecks from the Shangri-La list.

Sam hoped the GPS trackers would work.

He and Tom slowly made a short decompression stop, then ascended to the surface.

Sam used the last of his air to inflate his buoyancy control device so that it worked more like a life jacket than piece of diving equipment. Positively buoyant, he floated on his back, and looked up at the myriad of stars in the night's sky. Several constellations were already visible.

He switched on his personal locator beacon.

And on the horizon, he saw a flash, followed by the thunderclap of a distant explosion.

Chapter Thirty

Genevieve winched them out of the water twenty minutes later.

Still in his wetsuit, Sam dripped on board the *Tahila,* as Matthew confirmed Sam's worst fear. The illegal salvagers were using a strong GPS jamming device to block the signals from the GPS trackers they had placed on the *USS Houston.*

Sam said, "That's it then, they won. There's no way we're going to find that submarine now. They have their steel and they'll be able to build their antenna to locate Shangri-La."

"This antenna, do we have any idea what it would look like?"

"No," Sam said, "but the engineers I've discussed the concept with believe it would need to go on a large tower, focusing on a specific location."

"Does that mean they must already know the rough location?"

"It might mean that. But as you noted, Shangri-La could be anywhere in the world. If it is, there's no reason to believe that a tower would be able to pick up its position."

Veyron, entering the discussion, asked, "Do we know what it is that the antenna is searching for?"

"Not really. As far as we know, Shangri-La's still a mythical utopia."

"Only we now know it isn't a fictional fabrication, because someone's investing millions of dollars trying to locate it." Veyron considered the science and added, "The location must emit some sort of magnetic field, or something measurable, if someone believes they can detect it using low radiation steel."

Tom asked, "What's our next plan of action?"

Sam thought about that for a minute, then glanced at his friend. "You and I need to shower, change, and find food. Then I think it's time for all of us to come up with another way to reach the legendary lost lamasery."

Chapter Thirty-One

Sharing a slice of pepperoni pizza with Caliburn, Sam took a seat at the round table.

When the entire crew of the *Tahila* took their place, Sam asked, "What do we know about Shangri-La?"

Tom, swallowing a bite, said, "According to legend, if it's to be believed, it's a utopic lamasery hidden high in some secluded, near impossible to reach mountain range."

Genevieve laughed. "Of course, all of that comes from a fictional story written in the thirties."

Everyone's eyes turned to Sam, who shrugged. "Technically she's right."

"Come again?" Tom said.

"Everything we know about Shangri-La can be attributed to James Hilton, a 1930s novelist who famously wrote the novel, *Lost Horizon* – depicting a fictional isolated monastery, high in the Tibetan borderlands, where everyone was permanently happy."

Matthew wiped his mouth, his lips creasing into a broad grin. "Wait. You're telling me we're basing everything we know about this place on a 1930s work of fiction?"

"Afraid so," Sam admitted. "Hilton made the name part of history. At least six movies have been filmed about it, some named "Shangri-La," and others called "The Lost Horizon." Ever since he released his novel, it has become the byword for a mythical utopia, a permanently happy land, isolated from the world. But just because he wrote a fictional story about it, doesn't make it any less real."

Tom finished his third slice of pizza. Licking his lips, he repeated his previous statement. "Sorry, come again?"

"After the book was first published in 1933, it went on to win Hilton the prestigious *Hawthornden Prize* in 1934. Hilton is said to have been inspired to write *Lost Horizon*, and to invent "Shangri-La" by reading the National Geographic Magazine articles of Joseph Rock. He was an Austrian-American botanist and ethnologist exploring the southwestern Chinese provinces and Tibetan borderlands."

Genevieve's facial expressions displayed her fascination. "But you know that he didn't?"

Taking a large swig of Coke, Sam nodded. "Yes, according to Elise, who has been trying to track a series of encrypted communications from people she believes to have been Master Builders, there were several references to James Hilton's book back in the 1930s, and complaints that he'd given away secrets by exposing Shangri-La."

Veyron, the oldest member of the crew, said, "Millions of people have read Lost Horizon, myself included, and thousands have gone to the Tibetan highlands in search of the lost world, but no one has ever found it."

"No," Sam confirmed. "That's why Elise believed that Hilton never gave away the exact location. Instead, he revealed many specific facts about the place, suggesting that he had intimate knowledge of a world kept secret for thousands of years."

Tom's eyes widened with delight at the mystery. "So, Hilton visited Shangri-La – maybe he was involved in a plane crash or something – and then he returned to England, and decided to write a book about his journey?"

"Sure, makes sense," Genevieve agreed, pushing her plate away even though it had an untouched hunk of garlic bread on it. Tom snatched it up with a smile, but she ignored him. "But it doesn't answer why the Master Builders, who were so intent on keep the place hidden, would have ever allowed him to publish it?"

"My thoughts exactly!" Sam said, pouring himself another glass of Coke. "I actually spoke to Elise about this, and she had a different theory…"

Matthew asked, "Which was?"

Sam said, "Maybe *Lost Horizon* was both a fictional piece of literature, and a guidebook to those who knew of Shangri-La's existence."

Tom slipped Caliburn a slice of garlic bread, his lips thinning into a hard line. He wasn't buying any of it. "If that's the case, why hasn't anyone ever used it to locate the real utopia?"

"Elise believes that it required a code," Sam explained. "Specifically, it worked on a variation of the one-time-pad – the only truly unbreakable code in theory. To decode the message, a listener had to have both the book and the key."

Tom said, "You think the Master Builders have the cipher stored somewhere in their DNA?"

Sam spoke with a mouth full of pepperoni pizza, "It's a possibility."

Genevieve asked, "Okay, so what do we know?"

On the round table, Sam wiped his hands, then brought up a map of known locations that make reference to a near mythical place, isolated from society, in which all rulers could be governed. The table showed a 2D image of the Earth.

Sam pointed to each of the historical locations. "These are the earliest known references to places Elise believes might be Shangri-La."

One after the other, the monuments rose three dimensionally out of the two-dimensional map.

The Pyramid of Khufu – Egypt.

Temple of Artemis – Turkey.

Mausoleum at Halicarnassus – Turkey.

Statue of Zeus at Olympia – Greece

Colossus of Rhodes – Greece

Lighthouse of Alexandria – Egypt

Suppressing a belch, Tom ran his eyes across the names. They were all part of the Seven Ancient Wonders of the World. "Did any of them actually use the name Shangri-La?"

"No." Sam shook his head. "They didn't use any specific name, more just a reference to a place, isolated from civilization, where the greatest minds could live out their lives, ordained to rule and guide the known leaders of the world."

"Do they give any hint where this mythical place could be found?" Tom persisted.

"No, not at all." Sam circled a section of the map. "Elise has had a good look at it, but it does suggest that it must be somewhere within the classical antiquity and the Hellenistic world. These comprised the modern countries of Greece, Albania, Macedonia, Southern Italy including Sicily, southern France and south-eastern Spain, southern Ukraine, Turkey, Armenia, Azerbaijan, Syria, Lebanon, Israel, Jordan, Egypt, eastern Libya, Iraq, Iran, Afghanistan, much of Pakistan, plus a large slice of central Asia."

Tom gave a deep sigh. "Well, that narrows it a little. So, the Seven Ancient Wonders was like a roadmap?"

Sam's eyes narrowed. "I don't think so. I think it's more likely that the Master Builders who built many of the Ancient Wonders probably knew about Shangri-La, so left their own notes or reference to the utopia."

Tom was licking his fingers as he asked, "Wasn't that in a book somewhere?"

Genevieve nodded. "Yeah, one of those Ancient Wonders, archeological thrillers, by Michael Reilly... I think it was called the Seven Ancient Wonders or something?"

Sam grinned. "*Seven Ancient Wonders*, by Matthew Reilly – no relation to yours truly – the Australian author. A good read. It was based on what people think archeology is all about... Indiana Jones and all that."

Tom wasn't to be discouraged so easily. "Yeah, so?"

Sam said, "And yet you still think the Master Builders used the Seven Ancient Wonders to lead to Shangri-La?"

Tom nodded. "Sure, the best writers in the industry use actual archeology to base their stories."

Sam looked incredulous. "You think Matthew Reilly was onto something when he wrote an archeological thriller based on the Seven Ancient Wonders of the World?"

Tom shrugged. "Sure, why not?"

Sam grinned, shaking his head, still in disbelief that they were even entertaining this concept. "First off, Matthew Reilly's a thriller writer… doesn't he write those over the top action adventure books that are meant to be based on truth but are fanciful at best?"

Tom shrugged. "Hey, I don't mind reading them. What's your point?"

"His books are meant to be steeped in fiction."

"So?"

Sam sighed. "So, anything you're getting from his books won't be of use to us. And second, I read that book, he never mentioned anything about the Seven Ancient Wonders being a roadmap to Shangri-La!"

Genevieve said, "Besides, we're missing the fact that only six of the seven ancient wonders were ever found, or mentioned a place similar to Shangri-La."

"Actually, that's a good point." Sam steepled his fingers. "There's no archeological evidence that the *Hanging Gardens of Babylon* ever existed."

Tom asked, "If that's the case, why is it even included in the Seven Ancient Wonders?"

Sam said, "Because, despite a lack of any archeology evidence, the *Hanging Gardens of Babylon* have been described in detail by many notable Greek and Roman writers, including Strabo, Diodorus Siculus and Quintus Curtius Rufus."

Tom asked, "How did they describe it?"

"The *Hanging Gardens of Babylon* was said to be a remarkable feat of engineering with an ascending series of tiered gardens containing a wide variety of trees, shrubs, and vines, resembling a large green mountain constructed of mud bricks. It was said to have been built in the ancient city of Babylon, near present-day Hillah, Babil province, in Iraq."

"But there's no evidence it was real?"

"No."

"How do historians and archeologists explain that?"

"There are three theories. One – the descriptions were purely mythical, and the descriptions found in ancient Greek and Roman writings were a romantic ideal of an eastern garden. Two – they existed in Babylon, but were completely destroyed sometime around the first century AD. Three – the legend refers to a well-documented garden that the Assyrian King Sennacherib – 704–681 BC – built in his capital city of Nineveh on the River Tigris, near the modern city of Mosul."

Tom smiled. "Great, so we have a description of Shangri-La from a 1930s novelist, a few references to an isolated utopia on some of the Ancient Wonders of the World, and a fictional garden. It's not a lot to go on. We don't even know what we're looking for, do we?"

Sam said, "You were hoping for an image?"

"It might be something. Yeah, why do you have such a thing?"

"Not yet, but it's coming."

"Really? How?"

"Jordan says he's got an image of Shangri-La buried in his brain, as if implanted there by the Master Builders when he accessed the Obsidian Chamber."

Jordan was an eight-year-old kid. He had a unique condition called Autism Savant, which made him off the charts on the intelligence quotient, but almost non-existent on the emotional quotient scale.

Only a few weeks ago, Jordan had helped them locate the Obsidian Chamber, and in the process, Jordan's unique brain had linked with the origins of the Master Builders. In doing so, they had repaired parts of his brain, but also inserted memories from ancient Master Builders.

Tom asked, "I don't suppose he could show you?"

"He's in the process of painting it for me," Sam confirmed.

Tom tilted his head. "Painting?"

"Yeah, he said it's not like he can print a picture from his mind, but the image is real and its clear in his head." Tom clicked on his laptop. "He's going to email it to me... hang on, I'll check for it now."

Sam refreshed his mailbox. There was a new email from Jordan. He clicked the link and projected the image at the center of the round table.

Sam grinned. His eyes turning to Tom. "Remind you of anything?"

"No."

"Anyone?"

"Yeah, this," Matthew said, pulling up an internet search of a painting depicting the *Hanging Gardens of Babylon*.

They were pretty much an exact match.

Sam said, "I don't believe it."

Tom asked, "What?"

"The *Hanging Gardens of Babylon* is Shangri-La!" Sam's eyes widened. "What's more, I think Matthew Reilly might've been onto something. The Seven Ancient Wonders were an ancient roadmap to the lamasery, but only for those who were worthy."

Chapter Thirty-Two

After taking the plates away, Sam Reilly got Jordan on the line.

The gifted kid was projected onto the round table as a hologram, real Silicon Valley type of stuff. Sam had tried to convince Jordan to join his crew, but the kid wasn't interested. No how, no way. He might not technically be autistic anymore, but that didn't mean he wanted to become overly social either. He was content with his own company and a hermitic life.

Sam got straight to the point. "The *Hanging Gardens of Babylon* is Shangri-La!"

"Yes," Jordan confirmed.

"Does that mean it's in Iraq?"

"I doubt it."

"So why all the references to the *Hanging Gardens of Babylon* being in modern day Iraq?"

"My guess is that the entrance to one of the gateways was probably there. That's why there has been so much confusion over the years."

Sam's boyish smile flashed. "Gateways?"

The hologram of Jordan said, "Shangri-La is only accessible through a series of natural, spidery networks that open through specific gateways spread throughout the globe."

"You're telling me there was some sort of mythical gateway in Iraq, where people could travel there?"

"Yeah, pretty much."

"What happened to the gateway?"

"The same thing that happened to all of them." A slight smile flickered across Jordan's face. "It was most likely destroyed."

"Wait…" Sam said. "Let me get this straight, there's a network of tunnels, throughout the globe that link Master Builders to Shangri-La?"

"Yes. One in each continent."

Sam said, "But that would mean it must take months if not years to reach there!"

"No. It uses hyperloop technology."

"It uses hyperloop technology, as in Elon Musk's high-speed tunnel tube system?"

"Yeah, something like that. One for each continent. One gateway to enter the system."

"How could the ancient Master Builders have constructed something so advanced?"

Jordan gave a rueful laugh. "Everyone assumes the human race is at the peak of its evolutionary process – the most technologically advanced state we've ever reached."

Sam curbed a grin. "We're not?"

"Not even close."

"Really?"

Jordan said, "The Master Builders have been working with us for millions of years… they first built technology far advanced from what we have now."

"What happened to it?" Sam asked.

"Technological advancements aren't lineal. Think of them like a concertina…"

Sam tried to imagine that. "Go on."

"The original technology brought here by the Master Builders were constructed rapidly, but soon enough there just weren't enough people with the knowledge of how to build and maintain such advanced technology. Eventually the entire thing ended up collapsing. Now, slowly, humanity has evolved to the point where industrial science is becoming highly advanced once more."

"And this Shangri-La… this is the center of all of it?"

"Yes. It was the basis of the first Obsidian Chamber," Jordan confirmed. "That's where it all began, and why it's considered holy land. Despite the different factions between Master Builders it's sacred ground… a place where fighting is forbidden."

"So how do we reach it?"

"Shangri-La?" Jordan shook his head. "Nobody knows."

"You mean, these gateways might not even exist?"

"They exist, but most have been destroyed or lost."

Sam returned to the concept of the tunnels and gateways. "What are the tunnels made of?"

"Obsidian."

"And they spread around the globe?"

"Yes."

"How did the original Master Builders do that?"

Jordan paused, thinking about how he should answer that. It wasn't a case of not knowing, but more a struggle to understand how to simplify what he knew. "The Master Builders have an intricate relationship with volcanoes. They have technology that links with lava. That's why they work with obsidian. They can control it. Maneuver it at will. They have a specific type of nanotechnology that allows them to grow and manipulate the shape of obsidian."

"And these lava tubes spread out across the globe?"

"Yes. One for every continent." The hologram of Jordan became animated as he explained. "When the first Master Builders arrived at Shangri-La, a giant tree of lava tubes was grown, that spread over thousands upon thousands of years, across the globe in a spidery web."

"So how do we find these tubes?"

"That's a little bit more difficult… Now, the North American one was destroyed by George Washington, the Hellenistic one was ransacked by Alexander the Great, no one knows what happened to the tube entrance in Australia, Shackleton was searching for the one in Antarctica… The others have been lost over time or simply never found."

"If we could find one of these gateways, how does it work?"

Jordan said, "You want to know if you can just walk through it and come out the other side at Shangri-La?"

"Is that how it works?"

"No. The gateway needs to be activated."

"How do you do that?"

"There was a gateway made for each continent as a means of spreading the knowledge of the original Master Builders far and wide. There was one medallion made for each gateway, so that only the worthy could return."

Sam thought about the image he'd seen on the Chinese Shangri-La file. The one that depicted a snake chasing its tail. "The medallion's a key?"

"Basically."

"So now we need to not only find a lost gateway, but also one of the few remaining medallions?" Sam choked a laugh. "That doesn't sound too hard."

Jordan held the palms of his hands upward. "Hey, I'm not making the rules, just letting you know what I know."

Sam thought back to Ernest Shackleton's obsession with the South Pole. "Was Shackleton trying to reach one of these gateways?"

"It's highly possible."

"Then Shackleton must have had a medallion?"

"Yes, he did. In fact, you can see him wearing it at various events. It was something he wore everywhere, and yet one of the few things that served no apparent purpose."

Sam persisted. "What happened to it?"

"No one knows. It's not in any museum, which means it was probably passed down through the generations to his next of kin."

"I don't suppose he has any living relatives?"

The holographic image of Jordan began searching on his laptop, his fingers could be seen hammering the keyboard with the familiar staccato that Sam had seen Elise use when she tried to search for something for him.

A few seconds later, Jordan said, "Actually, according to Google it says, he does. A granddaughter. Alexandra Shackleton. I have a contact number, if you want to ask her."

Sam grinned. "Yes please."

Sam knew Alexandra Shackleton personally, after the great granddaughter of Ernest Shackleton had tracked him down to thank him for finding the Endurance, Ernest Shackleton's ship. He was confident that she would lend him the medallion.

Sam said, "Thanks for your help, Jordan."

"You're welcome. Anything else I can do for you?"

"No. That's it isn't it. There's no other way to reach Shangri-La, is there?"

Jordan paused. "Actually, there's one more way. Apparently, there was another gateway that's still active."

"Do you have the map?"

"Actually, I do, but it won't do you any good."

"Why not?"

"Because the map is for an eighth continent. Somewhere that has been flooded for thousands of years." Jordan made a dramatic, apologetic sigh. "So, unless you happen to know where the eighth continent is, you're all out of luck."

Sam grinned. "As a matter of fact, I happen to know it very well. What's more, I know someone who will help us get there."

Chapter Thirty-Three

The 8th Continent, Pacific Ocean

The US Air Force Lockheed C-5 Galaxy flew in a southeasterly direction until it reached a section of calm seas a few hundred miles east of New Zealand. The massive military cargo transporter had a high wing with a distinctive high T-tail vertical stabilizer fin. Its four TF39 turbofan engines were mounted on pylons beneath wings that were swept backward 25 degrees as it soared above the Pacific Ocean.

Above its plane-length cargo deck was an upper deck for flight operations and for seating 75 passengers, including the embarked loadmaster crew, all who faced to the rear of the aircraft during flight. Cargo bay doors could be fully opened at the nose and tail to enable heavy vehicles to drive through the fuselage for loading.

Sam Reilly sat in the additional third seat in the massive cockpit and stared through the windshield at the sea below. It turned from its distinctive midnight blue of deep ocean waters through to the rich azure of the relative shallows.

He smiled at the sight and shook his head. It seemed impossible that the vast submerged landmass of the 8th Continent had remained hidden for so many years. He closed his eyes and imagined the place that he and Tom had discovered not so long ago. It belonged in a Jules Verne novel – a secret world, buried beneath the sea. To access it, they needed to navigate a submersible into a large underground grotto that used to be a volcanic atoll, but in the past fifty years had sunk to a depth of eighty feet. The entire beach, protected by a strange obsidian dome, remained filled with air.

Around his neck rested a bronze colored medallion. In reality, it wasn't bronze at all, but an immensely more valuable metal alloy known as orichalcum that turned golden red in sunlight, but appeared old and tarnished at all other times. On its face stood two circles of serpents eating their tales, linked together to form the symbol of an ouroboros.

The Air Force pilot pointed to the GPS waypoint. It was flashing, indicating that they were in close proximity to their desired location. The pilot turned to Sam. "We'll be overhead in ten minutes. Are you happy in the water?"

Sam nodded. "Here will do. Thank you."

Sam left the cockpit, climbing down the steep set of internal stairs from the upper deck to the cargo deck below.

The loadmaster greeted him with a firm handshake. "Mr. Bower is already on board the Orcasub. He says the submarine's ready to be launched."

"Very good."

Sam followed the loadmaster aft, past an Apache helicopter and two Military ATVs, before opening up to where the yellow sports submersible had been secured. The cargo crew were in the process of removing the MB-2 tie-down devices, rated at 25,000 pounds capacity each, in preparation for the airdrop.

Sam glanced at the submersible. Normally in the realm of multimillion-dollar toys of billionaires, it had become his secondary underwater reliable workhorse.

The loadmaster met his eye. "Good luck, sir."

Sam said, "Thank you."

He climbed on board and secured the hatch before moving forward into the cockpit.

Inside, he ran his eyes across the control settings. The buoyancy controls were all set to negative, meaning that the Orcasub would sink as soon as it hit the water. The batteries were all full and the power was switched on. All air tanks were within their highest boundaries.

He reached down and attached his headset, adjusting the mike so that it sat just below his mouth. Sam said, "How are we looking, Tom?"

"We're all set. The bathymetric map is all ready, and programmed into the system. All you have to do is follow the directions."

"Thanks."

Tom said, "What about you?"

Sam suppressed the fear rising inside him like bile. "I remember the ride from last time. I'll be fine."

"Good man."

Up ahead, the aft cargo bay door opened vertically.

Cocooned inside the airtight and confined space of the Orcasub, he felt nothing of the strong gust of air that wisped around the inside of the C-5 Galaxy's cargo bay. The aircraft reduced altitude until it looked like it was setting up to land on the calm water above the 8th Continent.

The loadmaster gave the thumbs up signal.

Sam reciprocated the signal and then on the internal radio, he said to Tom, "Here's to hoping the jolt isn't as painful as last time."

"Can't be as bad as last time," Tom agreed, although Sam knew he'd enjoyed every minute of it last time.

The light next to the cargo open bay door turned from red to green.

Sam swallowed and pushed his body as hard into the seat as possible in an attempt to brace himself. The C-5 Galaxy flared just above the sea. A second later the loadmaster released the drogue chute. It shot through the cargo bay door and pulled the extraction chutes out into the airstream, opening fully with the loud crack of a whip.

The force of the extraction chutes immediately overcame the remaining floor lock, and the Orcasub was pulled out like the release of a catapult.

Sam's head jolted backward with the initial movement, but the landing was surprisingly soft, with the water absorbing much of the remaining force.

Behind them, the C-5 Galaxy was already climbing.

And the submarine began to sink.

Sam Reilly blinked, and regained his composure. "You okay, Tom?"

"Never better. I never tire of that ride."

The muscles in Sam's neck were already starting to feel tender with whiplash. He would never understand Tom's fascination with rollercoaster rides.

Sam said, "All right, let's get the show on the road."

He maneuvered the sports submarine with gentle, adept movements of the controls as he navigated the opening to the submerged world of the 8th Continent. The Orcasub was kind of a cross between an airplane and a two-seater submersible. Behind him, Tom Bower read out a series of intricate navigational details they had secured from their previous expedition, as a navigator would to a professional rally car driver.

The Orcasub set its course along a southwesterly direction through the remnants of an ancient submerged valley. Sam pulled back on the joystick, and the little submersible rose out of the higher cliffs of the nearly three-mile-wide valley, leveling out after its rapid ascent, across an ancient waterfall.

Emerging onto the tabletop of the 8th Continent.

Sam ran his eyes across the stunning vista. It had been nearly two years since he'd last been there, and nothing had changed.

The ancient river exited into a shallow underwater plateau, covered in vivid and impressive coral gardens. It was a unique tropical playground that didn't belong anywhere near where they were. Coral reefs provided homes for tropical fish, sponges, mollusks, giant manta rays, sea turtles, and giant clams. The diversity of form and color was the sort of thing that inspired humanity to explore beneath the waves in the first place.

Instead of dolphins playing with them, a pair of torpedo-like drones had found them and were tracking them as they made their approach.

That's different...

Sam slowed the Orcasub as he approached the end of the chasm, taking it to a stop at the mouth of a large underground chamber, roughly twenty feet high by thirty feet wide. He switched on the submarine's overhead lights, which shined like two little bug-eyes from the top of the sub. The cave formed out of the mouth of a small rocky outcrop on the coral tabletop, like an ancient monolith.

"You ready?" Sam asked.

Tom said, "Yeah. Take us in."

Sam dipped the joystick forward, and the Orcasub's propellers made a little whine as he edged her through the mouth of the opening.

The tunnel descended steeper until they were at a complete dive. At 160 feet, the rocky passageway appeared to level out, before ascending again.

At 140 feet the passageway opened, and seawater ceased. The submarine surfaced into a gigantic, air-filled grotto that extended so far back, that neither Sam nor Tom could see where it began or where it ended. A giant light filtered through the top of the cavern, like the rays of the sun, glistening onto the spectacular white beach.

Sam eased the Orcasub's throttles forward, until she became gently grounded on the sandy beach. Confident that the submarine was securely landed, Sam disengaged the hatch and climbed out. He removed his MP5 submachine gun and slung it over his shoulder. Tom climbed out second, carrying a rope and anchor behind him.

Sam fixed the anchor, burying it deep in the sand, while Tom attached the opposite end of the rope to a small retractable cleat on the Orcasub's starboard pontoon. After confirming the submarine was secured, they made their journey along the same well-worn path they had taken previously. They meandered toward the half-dome shaped remnants of the ancient volcano that now overhung part of the beach like the mouth of a behemoth monster turned grotto.

They passed the wooden remains of a 16th century Dutch Fluyt and the intact, well-preserved remains of Amelia Earhart's Electra. They quickly reached the three pieces of obsidian, each as large as a bus, that jolted together to form a natural archway, and began their descent into the unique world below.

Guarding the entrance to the unique underground world were two R2D2 Units. The Phalanx CIWS were a close-in weapon system for defense against airborne threats such as anti-ship missiles and helicopters. They would be capable of wreaking havoc against a submersible or anyone who dared to enter the beach.

Sam turned to Tom. "Those are new, too."

Instead of Tom, a woman answered.

It was Amelia Earhart. "I'm afraid they were a necessary evil to protect the inhabitants of the 8th Continent since its existence has become known."

She had blonde hair, which was cut short, and blew in the light breeze. She wore an impish smile, revealing a nice set of even white teeth, with a distinctive gap in the middle of her upper front incisors.

Sam smiled at her, broadly and without hesitation or restraint. "Amelia! It is so good to see you."

"You too, my friend." She embraced him with a firm hug. "It's going to be dark soon, we'd better get going if we're going to work out how to reach Shangri-La."

Chapter Thirty-Four

They stopped at Amelia's nearby cottage.

It seemed rudimentary, more of the sort of place where Robinson Crusoe might have lived – a single-roomed log hut, with a waterwheel fed by the nearby stream, and a garden of remarkable flowers. It was the epitome of a domesticated agricultural society. A small farm with a series of exotic fruit orchards, a level field, a nearby stream – its water being captured by a large waterwheel and redistributed to the orchards of exotic fruits – and a small cottage with a domesticated dog by the looks of things. Not quite what anyone would expect from the submerged prehistoric oasis.

Sam and Tom took a seat on her front deck, while Amelia poured all three of them a glass of whiskey. Sam thanked her and took a sip. From their vantage, he could take in the surreal environment of the 8th Continent.

The subterranean world was every bit as mythical and utopic as he'd imagined Shangri-La to be. His eyes swept the distant lands. The entire place was surrounded by a rocky vaulted ceiling so high that it could only be seen at the edges of the wall and not in the middle. A warm ray from the setting sun shone down from a distant horizon, giving the entire subterranean habitat a unique warmth, making him feel like he'd just stepped out into the great expanse of an ancient savannah. Giant trees and plants were covered with fruits filling his nostrils with the scent of rich fragrances.

His eyes swept the near-mythical environment with wonder. It was impossible to tell where the place began and where it ended. It might have been a small country in its own right. Thick rainforests, including giant gum trees, more than a hundred feet tall, filled the area. There were massive open plains of grass, and a freshwater river that split the ancient world in two, with multiple smaller tributaries and streams that ran off from it. An 80-foot waterfall raged somewhere to the east, sending a fine mist down upon the valley. The sound of birds chirping echoed throughout. Ancient megafauna, oversized mammals and marsupials, drank by the bank of the river.

Sam stirred the ice-cold rocks in his drink and took another sip. He brought Amelia Earhart up to speed about the Master Builders and the secrets of Shangri-La, explaining the need for their current urgency. That after maintaining the balance between good and evil for millennia, the old caretakers had recently died, leaving the world with an imbalance. Left untended to, there was currently a race to reach the ancient sanctuary and gain control over it.

Amelia wore the impish grin of a bystander watching a game for fools, which will ultimately have little effect over her life. "What will you do once you reach Shangri-La?"

"I don't know yet," Sam admitted. "My good friend Elise, who had descended from a long blood line of Master Builders, has recently traveled there to visit her parents who are currently trying to stave off a disaster."

"I don't see you ruling an isolated utopia. It sounds nice, but it's not your style."

"No," Sam agreed. "I want to make sure a new custodian is enthroned."

She arched her eyebrows. "And if you can't?"

Sam said, "Failing that, I think we need to permanently destroy the place."

Amelia mulled that over, as if considering whether to help or not – or even if it was the right thing to do. "All right," she finally said, "Show me this map you've been talking about."

Sam laid the map out on the table in front of her.

It depicted the central maze.

Sam pointed to the picture of the obsidian door at the center of the maze. "Do you know what's inside there?"

Amelia made a crisp reply. "No."

"Has anyone ever opened it?"

"Not that I know of… it's been locked for centuries."

"By who?"

Amelia shrugged. "I don't know exactly, but the caretaker of the maze said that it was locked by the ancient ones long ago."

Sam said, "I wonder how you unlock it?"

Amelia grinned. "That I can tell you, but you're not going to like it."

"Really?" Sam suppressed a smile. "How?"

"This world, you may remember from your previous journey, is made up of four quadrants. Summer, Winter, Fall, and Spring. The seasons in each quadrant never change, making it so that only Spring is habitable. In the middle of each quadrant there are large pyramids – temples, where the ancient ones you call the Master Builders once used to reside."

"I remember," Sam said, "What do we have to do?"

"There's a giant lever at the center of each of the four temples. You need to make certain the lever is set downward, instead of upward."

Sam arched his eyebrows. "That's all you have to do?"

"That's all, but like I said, no one's been to all four temples in centuries."

"How long would it take to reach on foot?"

"Months… maybe even years." Amelia grinned. "But I have a better idea."

Chapter Thirty-Five

Sam stared at the Cicaré CH-7 ultralight helicopter.

It was based on the single-seat Argentinian design from the late 1980s, later developed into a tandem two-seater. The piston engine-powered craft used the traditional "penny-farthing" layout with two-bladed main and tail rotors.

He turned to Amelia with a bemused smile. "You bought yourself an ultralight!"

"Yeah, I missed flying. I considered bringing in a fixed wing, but by the time I took off I would need to start looking for a landing space, and there isn't a lot of flat places to land anywhere on the 8th continent."

Sam asked, "How did you learn to fly it?"

"Learn to fly it?" She tilted her head, her lips pulling down at the corners. "I taught myself to fly it, after I put it together."

"You taught yourself to fly a helicopter?" Tom asked, his voice riddled with admiration.

She beamed. "Of course, I did. They haven't built an aircraft I couldn't figure out how to fly."

"I'm impressed," Sam said. "And an ultralight too. Those things are horribly unforgiving."

Sam ran his hands across the fuselage, studying the Cicaré CH-7 with joy.

The main rotor was constructed from composites and used a teetering, semi-rigid design with 6° of twist. The tail rotor was aluminum. The pod-and-boom fuselage had a fiberglass cabin built on a steel tube frame, with a long transparent forward-opening canopy. The steel frame carried the engine, semi-exposed behind the accommodation and connected it to the main rotor shaft by a belt drive. A slender aluminum boom, strengthened by a pair of long struts to the lower fuselage frame, carried both the tail rotor and swept fins.

To Amelia, Sam said, "She's a beautiful bird."

"Thank you, so do you think you or Tom will be able to fly her?"

"I'll work it out," Sam said.

She met his eye, holding his gaze. "Even though ultralights are horribly unforgiving?"

Sam shrugged. "I like flying."

Amelia turned to Tom. "What do you think, do I trust him?"

Tom curbed a slight grin. "Sam here spent six months as a teenager flying Robinson 22s in the Northern Territory of Australia, wrangling cattle. If there's anyone on Earth capable of handling an ultralight in these small confinements, it will be him."

She relaxed. "Okay. Well, she's fueled up, ready to go. Do you have a map of the 8th Continent?"

Sam shook his head. "We don't. Do you?"

"Yeah, I had a copy made from the one stored at the center of the maze."

Amelia withdrew a folded map of the strange lands.

There was a vertical line and a horizontal line through the middle, spitting the underground world into four separate quadrants of equal proportions.

She said, "Humans and most animals for that matter can live in the two northern quadrants. Fall in the northwest and spring in the northeast. For the most part, people choose to live here in the northeast."

"And the two southern quadrants?" Sam asked. "What do you know of them?"

"Animals do live there. Heck, even some humans have, but it takes a lot more effort and struggle to survive. You have to remember the seasons don't rotate down here, so summer is permanent and so is winter. In the south west, the land has hundreds of miles of scorching desert, a wasteland where almost nothing can survive, before ending in a land with a permanently active volcano – a place filled with lava lakes."

Amelia looked up at him, apparently waiting for some sort of challenge.

Sam merely waited in silent acceptance, before saying, "Go on. What about the winter quadrant?"

She sighed slowly. "The icy southeast quadrant is frozen all year round, with nearly a hundred miles of icy plains, before a high rising mountain."

"Have you ever been outside this quadrant?"

"I've been to the northwest, but never to the south." She met him with a leveled gaze. "If you survive, you'll be the first person in my lifetime to visit it and return."

Sam expelled a breath. "Well, here's to hoping we prove that stereotype wrong."

Chapter Thirty-Six

Sam thanked Amelia for the loan of her precious helicopter, promised to take good care of her, and then loaded their equipment into the tiny space behind their seats. He and Tom both carried small backpacks, with weapons and supplies for their journey. Having dealt with the large and deadly animals of the bizarre underworld previously, they opted to bring a pair of Remington V3 TAC-13 shotguns, loaded with 12-gauge buckshot, for maximum stopping power.

He took a seat at the pilot controls, shifting the chair all the way back.

Next to him, Tom crouched into the small cockpit, giving him the appearance of one of those clowns that climbs out of a tiny car at the circus. To Tom's credit, the veritable giant was surprisingly limber, and like all cave divers, seemed to appear well at ease in the most cramped of spaces.

A smile crept into Sam's eyes. "Are you comfortable?"

Tom appeared to relax into his seat, like a sloth, taking up every inch afforded to him. "Never better. I'm still interested to see what you can do with this bird."

"All right, let's see." Sam flicked the electrical switches to on.

The rotor blades began to turn. Slowly at first until they picked up momentum, and then they became nothing more than a barely visible whirr above their heads.

Sam waited until they reached 95 percent of their maximum RPMs. He set his right hand adeptly on the cyclic control and the balls of his feet nimbly on the peddles.

He gave Amelia a final wave goodbye and then with his left hand, he raised the collective control. The Cicaré CH-7 responded instantly.

The little ultralight took off like a sports car.

It took just a few seconds for the primitive part of Sam's brain to kick into gear, picking up the miniscule nuances of the small aircraft. Unlike the Eurocopter, which utilized its larger inertia to be more forgiving in its minor movements, the Cicaré CH-7 – with smaller inertia – responded to the tiniest incremental change in its controls. This made it much more difficult and dangerous to fly.

Even so, Sam Reilly had learned to fly on Robinson 22s, which weren't much larger, and it was all the same once you'd mastered the skills. Just like riding a bike. Only in this case, if you fall off, everyone dies.

Tom acted as navigator, reading out directions on the map.

Sam took the small craft up to 150 feet. He would have liked to fly higher, but the vaulted ceiling of the subterranean world didn't permit it. If anything, anywhere higher than that, and he would get a buffeting effect on his maneuverability due to wind on his rotor blades coming off the ceiling. These are similar to disturbances that impact flight near the ground and when hovering.

Tom offered him a compass bearing. Sam matched it, heading in a direct line for the pyramid at the spring quadrant. The Cicaré CH-7 settled into the straight and level flight to the farthest end of its world.

Sam watched the ground go by, enjoying the scenery. The 8th Continent was a startlingly beautiful place. With ancient trees that reached nearly to the ceiling, lakes and flowing rivers, their waters untouched by modern civilization were crystal clear. To the south, he spotted the skyway that he and Tom had traveled last time they visited.

The skyway was a series of linked bridges made of cordage rope that spanned the trees of the high rising forest, before reaching a treehouse built at the crest of an ancient Eucalyptus regnans nearly three hundred feet above the river.

The entire network spanned more than fifty miles. It had been created and used by nomadic travelers for centuries to avoid the strange world's numerous natural predators.

The thought of predators reminded Sam of the Haast's eagles. The massive predatory bird once lived in the South Island of New Zealand, and was commonly accepted as the Pouakai of Maori legend. The species was the largest eagle known to have existed. Its massive size was explained as an evolutionary response to the size of its prey, the flightless moa, the largest of which could weigh 510 pounds. In New Zealand, Haast's eagle became extinct around 1400, after the moa were hunted to extinction by the first Māori.

On the 8th Continent, the Haast's eagles were lethal toward humans, and had very nearly cost Sam and Tom their lives.

Sam swallowed at the thought of their last encounters with the deadly creatures, and was grateful to Amelia for loaning them the ultralight helicopter.

The entire flight took a little under an hour before they spotted the golden light reflect from the pyramidion.

Tom pointed to the pyramid.

Made of granite blocks, it stretched from the side of the riverbed, extending upward all the way to the top of the world.

In the front of the temple was a rectangular field of verdant grass, reminding Sam of a Mayan city. Sam banked the Cicaré CH-7 and landed on the foreground.

He switched off the engine and reached for the safety of his shotgun.

Unfolding himself out of the cockpit, Sam asked, "Shall we go explore the Temple of Spring?"

Chapter Thirty-Seven

The Temple of Spring looked like a cross between ancient Egyptian pyramid and Mayan pyramid in its construction. Unlike either pyramid, this one had a passageway that ran right through its center, along which water flowed freely.

It looked well maintained and for a moment, Sam half expected to see a Master Builder still residing within. But the pyramid had been long since deserted.

According to Amelia Earhart, none of the temples had been occupied for longer than any person's living memory. Within the mysterious world of the 8th Continent, people aged slowly. That could make it anywhere above 200 years since the temples had been permanently occupied by Master Builders.

Sam and Tom took their fully loaded shotguns with them as they walked up the first set of stairs, toward the main entrance. They weren't expecting any problems from humans. It was the other unknown predators they were concerned about and weren't willing to take any chances.

The entrance was an arched tunnel that extended to the center of the pyramid. A constant stream of water flowed into the pyramid through the bottom of the passageway, and a set of elevated masonry steps, formed a bridge above the water on which they could travel.

Light entered from well-placed openings within the temple, all the way through to its center. At the heart of the pyramid a large, solid bronze lever – roughly fifteen feet high – rose from the middle of the stream inside the passageway.

Sam stared at it. There were no markings to indicate which way the lever should go.

Tom bit his lower lip. "How do we know that we're shifting the lever in the right direction?"

Sam pointed to the water. "Amelia told me. She said that she had spoken to the caretaker of the maze – one of the oldest residents of this land. He gave her explicit instructions to unlock the obsidian door."

"So what were the instructions?"

"The waters of the four quadrants need to flow inward toward the maze."

Tom glanced at the water. "Right now, it's flowing outward, away from the maze."

"Exactly. And my guess is that as soon as we turn this lever, the water will begin to flow in the opposite direction."

"If it doesn't?"

"Then we need to come up with a new plan."

"All right."

Sam gripped the edge of the lever and tried to heave it across.

It didn't budge.

Tom cracked his fingers. "You want a hand?"

"Yes!"

Together they pulled the heavy lever.

It creaked as if accepting its submission and turned all the way to the right.

And nothing happened.

Tom said, "It didn't do anything."

"Give it time." Sam said, "Water doesn't change its flow instantly. It needs to overcome whatever obstacle we just produced, and then it will turn."

He hoped he was right.

About two minutes later, the water began to settle until it became still – the same way a slack-tide forms on the ocean.

And then the water began to retreat, heading away from the pyramid in the direction of the maze at the center of the four quadrants.

The lever turned a golden red.

Tom stared at it. "The lever was made out of orichalcum!"

"It would appear so. That just goes to show how old these constructions are. Orichalcum hasn't been used for nearly ten thousand years, since the Atlanteans were wiped out."

Sam watched the water flow in the opposite direction for a few minutes.

His lips parted into a half-grin. "One down, three to go."

Chapter Thirty-Eight

Amelia Earhart looked at the head of security.

The man was strangely short given his occupation, but extraordinarily solid, giving him an odd appearance, more like a battle dwarf one would expect to see in Tolkien's Middle Earth. The man's face was set with a disagreeable disposition, his eyes flashed genuine fear.

She asked, "What is it?"

"I'm sorry, Amelia. We've had an intruder."

"An intruder?" Her voice raised a pitch. Few people knew of the 8th Continent's existence, let alone how to overcome their state-of-the-art defense system. "How in the hell did that happen?"

The security officer turned his palms upward in a placating gesture. "We don't know, ma'am. We spotted the submarine, but when it arrived, no one was on board."

"Could it have been remotely operated and no one was on board?" she suggested.

"I'm afraid not. That's what we were hoping, but video footage later showed someone coming up out of the water, and racing along the beach, before entering the grand staircase and descending into the 8th Continent."

"How did he overcome the R2D2 CIWS?"

"That, we really don't know. It was like the automatic system recognized him."

"Do you have a photo of our intruder?"

The guard nodded, handing her his tablet.

She glanced at the image. It was a frozen frame from the video feed. The man appeared to be tall, with blond hair and dark purple eyes.

Amelia didn't recognize the man per se, but she knew that those eyes marked him as one of the so-called Ancient Ones.

It would explain how he'd managed to get past the R2D2 CIWS system. It was programed with all known residents of the 8th Continent, as documented by the caretaker from the maze.

The question remained, why had one of the Ancient Ones returned?

And more importantly, how she could get a message to Sam Reilly to warn him?

Chapter Thirty-Nine

The Cicaré CH-7 settled into its sweet spot, as it flew straight and level due west, at an altitude of 150 feet. Sam had become comfortable with the small craft's unique idiosyncrasies. He and the machine were working in perfect harmony, his brain and body making the hundreds of minor and incremental adjustments needed to keep the ultralight in the air.

Next to him, Tom was sound asleep. An old habit from their days in the military. Get rest while you can, because when the bad stuff hits the fan, you don't know when you'll get the chance again.

Sam continued flying, his mind on autopilot. Up ahead, he spotted the river that flowed north to south, dividing the quadrants down the middle.

He flew across the divider, leaving the spring quadrant for the fall quadrant – and immediately realized his mistake.

The Cicaré CH-7, was blown upward like a dragonfly in a storm. An updraft, like an air-curtain, split the two quadrants in half, preventing the temperatures from crossing between the quadrants to reach equilibrium.

Sam worked furiously to regain control of the helicopter. The yellow alert master alarm blared, indicating the rotor blades suddenly were not responding normally, the earsplitting warning adding to the confusion. The four long, flat, thin pieces of metal on top of the ultralight slowed.

Losing resistance on the blades, the engine loudly whined.

Sam throttled back.

The controls became floppy and unresponsive, as though they were no longer having to overcome the natural forces applied on them by the physics of gravity and aerodynamics. Sam's heart pounded in his chest, as he realized he was no longer a pilot, but merely a passenger unable to make any effect on the helicopter's flight.

The small craft flew toward the vaulted ceiling in an uncontrolled climb. Its tail spinning rotor stopped responding to his movements, and the craft started to fall in a deadly autorotation. The ultralight began to spin uncontrollably in a counterclockwise direction.

Sam planted his left foot on the pedal, and, seeing the ceiling race to greet him, he threw the collective all the way down, and pushed the joystick to its side – entering an intentional nosedive.

The helicopter turned on its side, plunging into a free fall.

The Cicaré CH-7 raced toward the ground on the fall quadrant side of the dividing river. As soon as they passed the air-curtain, the ultralight's controls abruptly became effective again.

Sam felt the controls, previously floppy, stiffen under the new forces. His eyes glanced at the altimeter. They were 100 feet off the ground. It wasn't a lot of room to regain control. The Cicaré CH-7 was spritely, and if anything could do it, this tiny helicopter would. He raised the collective, and tried to hold the craft steady in a nose upward angle. The helicopter raced to greet the ground, which was covered in large, autumn colored trees.

Beside him, Tom woke with a casual stretch. Like a kid on a rollercoaster, his face was set with practiced indifference, mixed with amusement. His eyes darted between the instruments and the ground racing to greet them.

"You got this, Sam?" Tom asked, meeting his friends panicked gaze.

The helicopter stabilized its fall, coming to a straight and level position of flight, cruising below the branches of a series of arched maple trees. It came out the other side, and Sam slowly increased his altitude until they were flying at 150 feet again. In the sweet spot. Ready to overcome any problems as they came up.

Sam expelled a deep breath. He could still hear his own blood pounding in the back of his head. He turned to Tom. "We're good."

Looking relaxed as all hell, Tom repositioned himself, returning to a comfortable position. He closed his eyes as though nothing had happened, and he was all set to go back to sleep.

Sam gave a rueful laugh. "Is that it?"

Tom rubbed his eyes. "Is what it?"

"You're just going to go back to sleep?"

Tom's eyes flashed a bemused smile. "Yeah. You said you had it under control, didn't you?"

"Don't you want to know what happened?"

Tom gave a noncommittal shrug. "I'm guessing you found some sort of powerful updraft when you crossed over the divider between the two quadrants. It rendered the controls all but useless until we had the good fortune to free fall out of it. Does that just about sum it up?"

A faint smile tugged at Sam's lips. "How did you know?"

"I had a guess. Actually, I was thinking about it earlier when we were flying. I was trying to rack my brains and work out how the four quadrants maintained their own weather patterns, without spilling across into the other quadrants to reach temperature equilibrium. I figured there must be some sort of air-curtain along the dividers to do so."

Sam shook his head. "You didn't think to mention this to me? We could have been killed!"

Tom readjusted his position. "Nah, I figured you'd have worked it out."

"You were counting on a lot of luck!"

"Hey, we're alive, aren't we?" Tom gave a wry laugh. "You always manage to figure things out on your own in the end."

Sam watched as Tom closed his eyes. Within seconds, his breathing had become the slow, relaxed breath of a person in a deep sleep.

He shook his head.

How much would he give to be able to fall asleep like that!

Chapter Forty

The Fall Temple was completely different to the Spring Temple. Instead of being made of granite, it was built out of wood, giving it a similar appearance and construction to something you would expect to find in Japan. Otherwise, it was still a pyramid, with a river that ran straight through the middle passageway.

If they'd had the time, Sam would have liked to study the design. As it stood, they were in a hurry. There was no way to know how long it would take the secret Chinese organization hell bent on finding Shangri-La to build their antenna, and to locate it. What's more, he still hadn't heard from Elise or Ben. Sam was beginning to worry that they hadn't reached Shangri-La or worse yet, had arrived and were in danger.

Either way, this wasn't a journey of archeological exploration. He needed to flick the correct bar, open the obsidian door, and make his way through the gateway to Shangri-La.

Tom pulled the lever and soon the water turned its direction, heading toward the center of the maze once more. Sam clambered into the Cicaré CH-7 and took off again, setting a course due south, to the Winter Temple.

As they approached the west to east running river that divided the northern quadrants from the southern, Sam brought the helicopter down low, hovering just five feet above the ground in front of the flowing water. After what happened last time, the notion of passing into another quadrant terrified him.

Sam looked at Tom. "Given that you managed to predict everything about the last air-curtain, do you have an idea how we cross it?"

A sardonic grin crept into Tom's eyes. "You seemed to handle it pretty well last time."

"I'm serious, Tom. How should we do this?"

"I don't know. Look, when you hit the updraft earlier, it sent us blowing toward the ceiling, right?"

"That's right," Sam confirmed.

"So, how about starting here, down low this time?"

"But then there's a good chance we're just going to lose lift at the critical time as we cross, and then what?"

"Then I suppose we crash into the river." Tom tilted his head sideways, trying to picture it. "If we are going to crash it'll be the safest way to do it."

"That's the best you've got for me?"

"Afraid so." Tom gave him a reassuring nod. "You'll be fine. You've survived six months Heli-wrangling, I'm willing to bet my life that you'll work it out."

"Thanks for the vote of confidence."

Sam eased the helicopter forward. He kept his hands and feet relaxed on the controls, ready to respond instantly to whatever reaction the air-curtain was going to have on them.

His rotor blades entered the updraft.

A split second later, the helicopter was blown forward and upward in the same sort of uncomfortable blast as before, they were back to being nothing more than a dragonfly in a storm.

Sam, ready for this response, immediately set about instigating the same series of maneuvers he initiated last time, designed to reduce lift, and cause the helicopter to stall.

It worked.

The ultralight, no longer providing any lift, fell from the clutches of the updraft. Sam adjusted the controls, trying to make certain he fell on the southern side of the river. His arms and legs worked furiously to regain control of the aircraft.

And then, just like that, the helicopter reached the other side.

Sam felt the controls, previously floppy, stiffen under the new forces. His eyes glanced at the altimeter. They were just 50 feet off the ground this time, even less room to regain control than before.

But the air was freezing.

Cold air was good for flying. Cold air meant denser air, which improved both airlift and engine performance. With more air getting into the cylinders, and a greater mass of fuel-air mixture, the helicopter had more stability.

The little craft recovered quicker than last time.

He raised the collective, attempting to hold the helicopter steady in a nose upward angle. It responded perfectly. More like the spritely helicopter that Sam had expected it to be.

"Nicely done," Tom said. "A few more of these and you'll have this all down pat."

"Yeah, two more to go and we'll be back at the maze."

They soon settled into a standard straight and level flight.

Sam, no longer pressured by time, allowed his eyes to wander, taking in the new scenery of this strange land of ice and snow.

The entire territory was white.

The ground a flat sheet of snow and ice, it might as well be the North Pole in the midst of winter. There were no mountains, no animals, and the few trees that existed, looked like they had been dead for centuries.

After twenty minutes, the shimmer of sunlight reflected off something in the distance. Sam's eyes narrowed, taking it in.

They flew a little farther.

Sam released the whisper of a gasp, as his eyes landed on the Winter Temple.

It was an identical pyramid to the two previous ones in size and shape, but instead of granite or wood, the entire building had been constructed of solid blocks of ice. Flowing through the passageway in the middle of the temple was a river of ice. It appeared to be slowly moving like an ancient glacial stream.

Chapter Forty-One

Sam put the Cicaré CH-7 down on a frozen lake.

He tentatively eased the pressure off the rotor blades, letting the helicopter's skids dig into the ice. Sam bit his lower lip, searching the ice for signs of cracks or fractures. Any indication that the whole area was about to give way. The last thing they wanted now was to lose the helicopter and be trapped in the frozen grounds of the Winter Temple.

"What do you think, Tom?"

Tom gave a non-committal shrug. "It'll probably hold."

Sam gave it another minute, then with an air of fatality, he switched off the master controls. The pitch of the rotor blades turned from a screeching whine to silence, as they slowly coasted to a stop. They got out, grabbed their weapons, but by now were feeling less threatened by the bizarre world they had been traveling through. Even so, they weren't taking any risks.

The ground beneath Sam's *Scarpa Terra GTX* hiking boots was slippery. Their rubber soles, designed for gripping rock, barely caught any purchase on the ice. Sam nearly went over, catching himself at the last moment.

Tom met his gaze. "You okay?"

"Fine. It's just like ice skating."

"Are you any good at that?"

Sam shook his head. "Not really."

"It shows," Tom observed dryly, making Sam give a snort of laughter.

Tom began a confident stride across the ice toward the entrance of the Winter Temple. Despite his size, he always seemed to be sure-footed. Sam's competitive streak triggered and he quickly caught up, making the effort to widen his stance, and keep moving. It was only when he tried to stop or change direction that he found himself nearly falling.

They reached the entrance to the pyramid.

An ice flow with similar properties as a glacier appeared to have been slowly shifting in the direction of the pyramid for what must be centuries. Inch by inch, it maintained a barely perceptible movement of flowing ice. Above the frozen river, large shards of ice blocks had been carved into the side of the pyramid. This created a walkway of stepping stones – or in this case, stepping ice – roughly three feet above the river.

The ice river below looked solid enough, but neither of them wanted to take a chance at falling through. The ambient temperature was low enough to kill without adding water to the equation. Sam climbed up onto the first ice step.

He cautiously placed one foot on the next one, followed by another. He tried to hook the heel of his boot on the rigid edge of the block, the only place he could gain purchase without slipping off completely.

It was an extraordinarily difficult juggling act, but he was making it work.

Sam spotted the lever up ahead. Maybe another forty feet away. He was going to make it. The thought encouraged him to pick up his pace. He found if he didn't pause between steps, he could keep a sort of balanced momentum going that helped him stay balanced.

Until it didn't.

His left foot missed the groove in the step, causing it to slip out from under him. One second upright and in control. The next, it was the opposite.

As he fell, he knew he had no chance of recovering from the fall. Instead, he worked to mitigate the damage. He turned to his side, trying to brace himself with his arms.

And landed hard on the ice river.

The fall sent pain shooting right across his body. It was so bad he couldn't comprehend exactly where it hurt. He felt the muscles in his abdomen spasm, pulling on his stitches, but even that didn't feel exceptionally painful compared to the agony in the rest of his body.

Tom held his breath, in sympathetic pain. "Are you all right?"

Sam expelled a breath. He didn't even realize he'd been subconsciously holding it after the hit to his ribs had knocked the wind out of him.

He slowly, carefully picked himself up.

Everything worked, and although he would have some new bruises, Sam intrinsically knew he would be okay. Nothing vitally important was broken.

He fiercely bit down on his urge to groan. "I'll be fine."

Tom stared at the river, looking for signs of cracks or damage. Finding none, he softly lowered himself down to the glacier passageway.

"You're going to have a go at the ice steps?" Sam suppressed a smile. "See if you can do any better than me and all that?"

Tom walked comfortably up to the lever. "No, I'm good. No reason not to learn from your mistake."

Together they pulled the lever.

There was no noticeable difference to the ice flow, but Sam felt confident it had worked. Ice moved slowly. There would be no visual clues for days.

He stared at the ice.

For an instant, he wondered if he could see the start of fine hairline cracks begin to form. It was as though the ice, having changed direction, was now starting to crack from the backflow.

Either way, he and Tom weren't going to wait around to find out.

They headed back to the helicopter.

As they were getting in, Tom said, "Look at your two o'clock."

Sam's eyes darted up ahead and slightly to the right.

There was a polar bear.

Sam whispered. "What the hell is a polar bear doing here?"

It appeared to be uninterested in them, so neither he nor Tom reached for their weapons. None of it made sense though. Polar bears existed in the northern hemisphere. There was never any history of them living this far south, even if a near mythical place such as the 8th Continent existed, with a permanently frozen region.

Tom shrugged. "Beats me."

They climbed into the helicopter.

Tom said, "Look out there! At your four o'clock! There's a man out there."

Sam glanced at the man.

The man was tall, with long gray hair and a matching salt and pepper beard that extended all the way down to his narrow waist. He wore a perfect white cape, and carried a long staff, giving him the appearance of a wizard.

Sam stepped out of the helicopter and waved at the man. He shouted, "Hello."

The ghost of a smile appeared on the man's face, before he turned and walked away.

Sam stood up, prepared to go after the stranger.

"Leave him," Tom said, stopping him with a hand on his shoulder. "That guy's probably a recluse who's lived here for more than a century. We've probably just frightened him."

"I'd still like to talk to him. Amelia said that no one had been to these regions in living memory. But here we are with living, breathing, proof that someone has."

"Even so, it's not for us to chase him. Besides, look." He pointed. "That polar bear is tracking him."

Sam's eyes narrowed. The man continued walking out into the ice. Next to him the polar bear approached. He placed a single, affectionate hand on the massive creature, and the polar bear tamely followed beside him.

"The old man has tamed a polar bear." Tom beamed with pleasure. "Well, now I've seen it all."

"Yeah, you and me both," Sam agreed. "Who doesn't want a pet polar bear? All right, three down, one more to go."

Chapter Forty-Two

They crossed over the third divider air-curtain without incident, and headed into the summer quadrant. The heat hit Sam like a wave of fire. It was the dry heat of a rocky desert. Sam brought the helicopter under control and set a course for the final pyramid – the Summer Temple.

His eyes swept the new region with fascination and awe in equal proportions.

The region near the river reminded Sam of the rocky desert of Moab in Utah. There were a multitude of delicate stone archways, big enough for him to fly through, rocky towers, and a labyrinthian warren of stone caves, pinnacles, tunnels, and boulders.

They flew across the vast desert, before spotting the ancient pyramid.

It was constructed at the base of a large overhanging cliff wall. The pyramid reminded Sam of the type of ancient architecture used by the Ancestral Puebloans. These people once lived in the present Four Corners region of the United States, comprising southeastern Utah, northeastern Arizona, northwestern New Mexico, and southwestern Colorado.

The pyramid was carved into the rocky cliff-face, with its outer façade constructed mainly of sandstone blocks plastered together with mud and mortar.

Sam put the helicopter down on top of a platform made of stones. He shut down the ultralight, grabbed his weapon, and said to Tom, "Last one to go."

Tom nodded. "Let's make it a good one."

The passageway into the temple looked identical to the other three with steps carved into the side of the wall above the river. Only in this case, the river had turned dry long ago. In its place, a searing fiery wind ripped through the passageway.

Sam knelt down at the river's edge, dipping his hand into the empty river. He instantly yanked his hand back, shaking it for a few seconds afterward.

Tom's mouth opened, surprised. "What is it?"

"The wind. It burns like fire."

Tom glanced at the stone steps that formed their pathway to the lever at the center of the pyramid. His eyes darted between the artificial skyway and Sam. "In that case, I'd suggest refraining from falling in this time."

"Agreed," Sam said, his mood lighter than what it should be.

He was steady on his feet when ice wasn't involved, but even so, Sam didn't kid himself. The fact remained – one false move, a single slip, and he'd probably burn to death inside a fiery invisible river of wind.

They carefully jumped from stone ledge to stone step until they reached the lever. Presenting no surprises, it was easy to shift it. Once again, nothing appeared to happen immediately. Yet a minute later, the wind changed direction, its searing heat now flowing from the pyramid inward toward the maze.

Sam watched the remarkable phenomenon for a few minutes.

Afterward, he turned to Tom and said, "That's four down. Let's open the obsidian door. It's time to visit Shangri-La."

Chapter Forty-Three

Amelia Earhart ran down the rocky pathway.

She was breathing hard, her chest burned, and the muscles of her legs ached. But she wouldn't stop, not even for a few minutes of rest. She kept a second helicopter at the community farm so that she could help locate injured animals from the air. It was the only way she would be able to reach Sam and Tom before they entered the maze.

And she urgently needed to reach them.

Amelia had to warn them that one of the Ancient Ones had returned. Even with her helicopter, she might be too late. Amelia closed her eyes, picturing Sam and Tom in her little Cicaré CH-7. They were making their way around the quadrants in a counter-clockwise direction.

It was going to be close.

She thought about her second helicopter waiting for her. The one she liked to fly for pure pleasure. It was a Mosquito XE with an open airframe. The XE airframe was a unibody construction resulting in a single structural element, offering aerodynamic cleanliness and good looks. This one was painted bright purple. Amelia didn't have any particular sense of favoritism for that color, except at night when the iridescent birds seemed to respond to the purple and fly beside her.

It was such an extraordinary experience, she decided to keep the color.

The helicopter was powered by a Compact Radial Engine MZ202. The two-cylinder, two stroke had a maximum power output of 64hp, ample to do the work for its 610lbs of gross weight. All in all, it was a dream to fly, bringing her as close to the elements of real flight that any human could achieve.

Amelia reached the barn and rolled open the hangar door. As soon as she looked inside, she swore.

Someone had stolen her aircraft.

The door was never locked. Why would it need to be? After all, she was the only person on the 8th Continent who knew how to fly a helicopter.

Her mind returned to their recent intruder.

Could the Ancient One have stolen it?

If he had, that would mean only one thing.

Sam and Tom were in big trouble.

Chapter Forty-Four

Sam kept the helicopter flying straight and level.

The shadow of the craft raced across the labyrinthian warren of stone caves, pinnacles, tunnels, and boulders below. Up ahead, a massive stone archway greeted him. Sam restrained himself from the nearly overwhelming urge to fly the helicopter straight through the guts of it. Even he knew some risks were too great to take just for the sake of it.

He was feeling good. They had achieved the near impossible by visiting all four quadrant temples and flicking the ancient Master Builder levers. He could land inside the center of the maze, enter the now unlocked obsidian door, and take a trip to Shangri-La.

The sun was dipping and the shadows along the ground were getting longer. The shadow of their ultralight seemed to be elongating to the point that it was looking like a different helicopter altogether.

Sam kept finding himself watching it, trying to determine how the dipping sun altered its natural appearance. Then it seemed to change shape again. It grew, becoming more like a giant blob of helicopters.

His brow furrowed with puzzlement.

Unable to work out what was making the strange changes to the shadow, Sam felt the need to alter the helicopter's position.

Sam altered his course, shifting briefly to their left.

He watched the shadowy blob widen.

The shadow's response mystified him. Why would it stretch out, and then turn into a blob again? It made more sense that the entire blob should shift to the left. Whereas, in his case, the shadow shifted, and then the original one moved to catch up before joining him.

Sam tried going the other way and got the exact same response.

Tom looked at him. "Are you okay? Something bothering you?"

A sheepish grin creased Sam's lip. "I don't know. I'm just a little concerned about our shadow."

"Okay… that makes sense," Tom said, returning to his topographical map.

Sam made a quick dash to the left, returning them to straight and level flight, on a direct course for the maze.

Tom put the map down. "All right, that's kind of getting annoying. What exactly is it about the shadow that's disturbing you?"

Sam's lips thinned into a hard line. "I'll show you."

Sam repeated his previous maneuver.

The shadow widened, before the original mass of darkness caught up.

"See!" Sam said, "Why is there a delay? A shadow is based on light being blocked. Therefore, it should travel at the speed of light. Ergo, we shouldn't view even a second delay in its movement. Definitely no lag like we're seeing there!"

"Oh, okay… that's interesting," Tom said, in a way that suggested it was anything but.

"Do you have an explanation?"

"No. The only thing I could think of was if there was a second helicopter near us. Maybe trying to hide its shadow in ours."

A chill of fear passed over him, like the darkness of evil stalking them.

Both men turned around, searching.

Behind them, matching their exact speed, was a Mosquito XE ultralight helicopter. In its single seat, was a man with blond hair.

There was raw fury and malice in the stranger's expression.

"Watch out!" Tom called, "He's got a gun!"

Chapter Forty-Five

The gunshot report pierced the sky.

The sound of it was strangely amplified by the disruption of the otherwise monotonous drone of the helicopter's rotor blades.

Sam banked to the left and dipped the nose of the helicopter downward, spinning wildly through the massive stone archway. The gap was so narrow that the ultralight only just fit through the middle by flying over on its side. Once on the other side of the arch, Sam pulled the helicopter back up, running so low between a series of rocky pinnacles that its rotor blades nearly sliced the top of the rocks.

Their attacker tracked them, mirroring their movements, following them through the stone archway and descending into the canyon far below.

"He's still on our tail!" Tom warned.

"I'm on it!" Sam said, already plotting his next trick.

Another two shots fired. The first shot fell short, hitting the boulder to their side, a small plume of dust showing where it struck. The second one landed on the side of their domed windshield, causing the Perspex to splinter into a localized star.

Tom said, "Get out of his line of sight!"

"I'm trying!"

Sam increased their speed, and swung around a series of boulders, before climbing above a mesa. On the straight and level, it didn't take long for their pursuer to reach them and begin taking shots again.

The problem was that the Mosquito XE helicopter didn't have a bubble-dome, only a small windshield. This meant the attacker was free to take a shot at them whenever he liked, whereas it would be near impossible for Tom to shoot out of the little ventilation holes. To even attempt to make such a shot, Sam would need to bank the helicopter so that Tom was perpendicular to their assailant – a feat made impossible in the narrow confines of their flight.

Sam spotted another deep canyon.

He banked the helicopter around to the right, dipping below a stone arch that marked the canyon's entrance. Flying at speed, he traveled through another three arches that progressively increased in size, until the canyon turned into a large predominantly covered cave system. Light shined through the gaps, but none of the openings were large enough for the helicopter to escape to the surface.

Sam swallowed hard.

They were committed now.

Sam glanced at Tom's face, which, for the first time in his memory, displayed Tom's discomfort. The whites of his knuckles were showing as he gripped the side of his seat. His folded navigation map now firmly placed in his thigh pocket.

Neither men spoke.

Every speck of Sam's focus and concentration needed to be on flying the ultralight. Even the smallest of interruptions could cost them their lives. Swinging around, he dropped deeper into the cave, ripping through the narrow confines.

"Do you see him?"

"I've got nothing!" Tom replied, searching their rear.

"Hold on, I'm going to bring us around."

Tom braced against the edge of the domed canopy, and reached back for the Remington V3 TAC-13 shotgun. He slid open the large air vents that allowed him to bring the shotgun's barrel out of the Perspex windshield.

Still inside the cave, Sam spotted what appeared to be a deep sinkhole.

He brought the helicopter into a hover, holding it directly above the ancient limestone cavity. He lowered the aircraft down until its rotors were well below the surface of the cave system.

They both held their breath.

Nothing happened.

Tom glanced around the domed canopy, searching for the Mosquito XE, while Sam used every synapse his brain could muster to keep the helicopter from crashing into rock walls.

Time passed interminably slowly.

Sam couldn't take it. "Where did he go?"

Tom shook his head. "No idea. He's not up there. Maybe he's not a risk-taking psychopath who refuses to be drawn into flying inside a cave system with a maniac?"

Sam grinned. "Hey, you said you wanted to see what I could do with the Cicaré CH-7!"

"Touché! But when I said that, I wasn't expecting you to take us caving inside the damned thing!"

Sam tried to feign his habitual insouciance, but it fell short. "Hey, I wasn't expecting to get shot at today, so what are you going to do?"

"Now what?"

"I don't know. It's not like I can hover here indefinitely."

"Maybe give it another thirty seconds, then leave?" Tom suggested. "Who knows. Maybe we've lost him?"

"Sound like a plan."

They reached thirty seconds and Sam glanced upward, ready to climb out of the prehistoric sinkhole. Above them, the Mosquito XE flew past them overhead.

Sam cursed. "That was close."

Tom recovered first. "Quick, after him! If I can get a shot out, we can take him down."

Sam's fight or flight system kicked in. This was their chance to finish the battle once and for all. He climbed the helicopter out of the sinkhole, following the Mosquito XE. Sam found their attacker's tail and began the chase.

His eyes flashed respect for the pilot as he watched the Mosquito XE navigate the narrow cave system. It confirmed to him that the man was a Master Builder. He had to be. Lightning fast reflexes was a strong genetic marker in those descended from the ancient Master Builder DNA. As he watched the pilot outpace him, Sam became certain that a normal human was incapable of making the maneuvers at such speed.

Tom urged him on. "Keep up with him!"

"I'm trying!"

The cave system dropped again, and the ambient light darkened. Sam struggled to see the walls. Instead, he focused on the Mosquito XE, trying to keep the Cicaré CH-7 in line with it. Still marveling at the other pilot's skill, Sam forced the dogged little craft to keep up.

Tom kept the shotgun barrel aimed through the open vent, ready to take a shot as soon as it lined up with their attacker.

Up ahead, the faint glow of light began to expand.

They were coming to the end of the tunnel, the outside world fast approaching. Sam swore. The cave appeared to narrow at the end.

One of the Mosquito XE's rotor blades clipped the edge of the cave wall. Sparks flew, but the small craft's momentum carried it through.

And out into the open world on the other side.

Sam couldn't see what happened to the enemy's helicopter. Not that it mattered. He needed every single thought process available to concentrate on piloting the Cicaré CH-7.

It was too late to slow the helicopter.

He needed the momentum to bank as he approached the exit. It was the only way to bypass the narrow opening.

His little craft raced through, its rotor blades mere inches away from the stone wall that enveloped them. Its whining engine echoing in the confined space of the enclosed cavern. Sam's heart rapped in his chest, as he tried to bite down on the rising fear.

And then their helicopter was outside.

In the open air, Sam and Tom exhaled a sigh of relief.

Below them, they spotted the wreckage of the Mosquito XE where it crashed near the entrance, skidding to the edge of the river.

The river!

An intense sense of threat triggered Sam's hindbrain and medulla oblongata – that primal part of the brain that deals with survival responses. It was warning him of an immediate danger.

Something about the river.

"The river!" Sam shouted, but it was too late.

They crossed the dividing waterway at full speed.

The sudden updraft caught them as they banked on their side, sending their ultralight into a deadly autorotation. Sam fought with the controls but was unable to make the machine work for him.

He had no chance of regaining control.

The helicopter floundered, and struck the shallow water on the opposite bank of the river. It skimmed for a split second before its rotor blade dug into the sandy bottom. Then the Cicaré CH-7 slammed into the water hard.

Chapter Forty-Six

Sam gasped in a last breath of air, just as the helicopter went under.

He reached for his seatbelt clip, but turbid water and bubbles filled the cockpit, rendering it impossible to see a thing. He found it by feel and coolly unclipped it. It took no time at all for Sam to extricate himself from a watery death.

The entire event felt familiar, and no wonder.

Strangely enough, this wasn't Sam's first downed helicopter he'd had to escape after it crash-landed into a body of water. Even more recently, he and Tom had fled a sinking Dodge pickup.

Practice does indeed make perfect.

The water was shallow, and by the time Sam had clambered out the hatch to the domed canopy, his head was already breaking the surface of the river.

He took in a deep breath.

And turned to look for Tom.

A small part of the helicopter was sitting out of the water, but apart from that there was nothing but river to be seen.

"Tom!" he shouted.

His eyes scanned the crash zone and the nearby river for any signs of his friend. If Tom had made it out of the aircraft, he hadn't yet reached the surface.

Sam took a couple deep breaths, grabbed his knife, and returned to the submerged wreckage.

The bubbles were settling, and he could just make out the sight of Tom, sitting in his chair. His seatbelt had become caught in a bent section of the craft, making it impossible to unclip. Tom's arms were folded across his chest. Calmly waiting, he somehow wore an unconcerned expression across his face, that suggested he knew all along that Sam wouldn't leave him there all day.

Sam went to work quickly, slicing the polyester seatbelt and pulling Tom through the open door.

On the surface his friend took several deep breaths.

The color returned to Tom's face. His mouth spread into a broad grin. "Much appreciated, Sam. Maybe next time feel free not to leave me down there so long though. I was starting to feel a little out of breath."

Sam matched his grin. "I'll take it under advisement."

On the opposite side of the river, their attacker, stumbling and dazed from his crash – pulled out his handgun. He aimed it at them, and shouted, "Don't move!"

Chapter Forty-Seven

Sam dived under the water, slowly coming up on the opposite side of the partially submerged helicopter. Tom was right there beside him.

He always wondered why people called out "Don't move!" when they needed their intended to hold still so they could shoot them. Does anyone ever listen to such a request?

He exchanged a glance with Tom. The river was wide. Probably somewhere in the vicinity of two-hundred-and-fifty feet and fast flowing in the middle. It would take an exceptionally strong swimmer to successfully cross it.

Sam asked, "What do you think?"

"I think our friend there is all out of luck. There's no way he's going to hit us from there. He has a handgun, but we have shotguns. It would take serious effort for him to swim across. No way he's going to do that and still aim a gun."

"Agreed." Sam shook off his worry. "Even if he tries, we'll easily pick him off with a well-placed shotgun round."

"All right, let's grab our stuff from the helicopter and keep moving."

"Okay, any idea how close we are to the maze?"

Tom gave it some thought. "We're probably somewhere between thirty and forty miles east of the maze. At least we're on the right side of the river."

"Yeah, that's something."

They made a quick dive, retrieving their backpacks and weapons.

The Remington V3 TAC-13 shotguns probably didn't like the drink, but they would fire well enough for the time being.

Equipped with the few supplies they had, Sam and Tom began to walk west. Their attacker, still on the opposite side of the river, continued to stalk them. He'd put his handgun away, having accepted that it would be near impossible to get lucky and hit both of them. Their pursuer had decided to save his ammunition for a better shot in the future.

Sam and Tom kept pace with each other, each one trying to set a decent speed. They knew that somewhere along the way, they would need to lose the man who was tracking them with an intent to kill.

The question was how and when?

An hour later, something on the riverbank caught Sam's attention. It was partially afloat, with half of it out of the water on the bank, and the other half still floating. His gaze locked onto it.

He beamed with pleasure. "Hey, is that a raft?"

They ran to the small floating platform. It was rudimentary in design. Just four logs tied together with some sort of cordage made of bark.

Tom said, "Welcome to our Deus-ex-machina."

Chapter Forty-Eight

They pushed the raft out into the fast-flowing middle of the river and climbed aboard. The raft caught hold of the current, and began to quickly pick up speed. They gave a friendly wave to their attacker, who fruitlessly sprinted to keep up. To their delight, they soon lost sight of him in their wake.

After twenty minutes they spotted a couple huge birds of prey soaring in the thermals high above. Sam watched them with a wary gaze.

The birds watched him too.

Sam said, "I've seen those huge feathered creatures before."

"Did you run 'a fowl' of them?" Tom quipped.

"Very funny." Sam smiled. "These fellows are beautiful, but also dangerous. They were called Haast's eagles, originally native to New Zealand, they were thought to be extinct until their recent discovery on the 8th Continent. They're known to descend at a freefall like a bomb being dropped from a plane high above, ripping up its prey with razor sharp talons a quarter of a foot in length."

After ten minutes, the prospect of two defenseless humans apparently became too much for the predators to pass up. One of the oversized eagles set up for the attack. Its huge wings arched backward, and it began to dive, its velocity rising with every second. It was followed by the two other opportunistic birds.

Sam and Tom both aimed their shotguns at the eagle that was far ahead of the others.

They waited until it got in close.

Sam squeezed the trigger first, followed by Tom a split second later.

The large 12-gauge buckshot ripped into the bird, turning it to a mixture of blood and exploding feathers. The bird never pulled out of its dive, crashing hard into the side of the raft, killing it instantly.

"Sorry, buddy," Sam apologized, then he fired another shot just to make some noise. The two other predators having learned their lesson, flew away at speed.

Tom said, "Smart birds."

"Yeah, smart us as well for bringing buckshot."

They continued to float down the river.

The sun set and the Haast's eagles, which dominated the sky in the day retired for the night. In their place, strange blue bioluminescent birds rose up from the forest, lighting the night sky with a constellation every bit as spectacular as the stars seen from above ground. As the velvet darkness of night took over, the obsidian grotto turned into a vibrant constellation of blue-green stars. Sam relaxed onto his back on the raft and stared up at the myriad of moving incandescent blue birds as they appeared like shooting stars throughout a galaxy of green glowworms.

Not long now until they reached the entrance to the maze

Chapter Forty-Nine

The Maze, 8th Continent

The next morning Sam awoke to the dark purple light of predawn, as it broke the velvet night's sky.

In the distance a series of high-pitched growls indicated they had reached the maze. Sam recalled that last time they were here, the maze was home to a pride of marsupial lions. The apex predators weren't anywhere near as large as their African counterpart, but they were deadly enough. Their Heckler and Koch MP5 submachine guns had struggled to stop them.

This time, it would be different.

This time they were armed with a pair of Remington V3 TAC-13 shotguns, loaded with 12-gauge buckshot for maximum stopping power. Even so, they wouldn't have enough rounds to kill them all. Sam was hopeful that the sound would be enough of a deterrent.

They pulled up their raft along the bank of the river, loaded their backpacks, checked their weapons, and made the short hike to the entrance of the maze.

The growls got louder now, echoing throughout the obsidian walls.

Sam stopped at the entrance.

He and Tom had made their way through the maze previously, and already he was concerned about how it would behave. Although it wasn't actually alive, it felt very much so. A series of underground aqueducts acted like hydraulics on the maze's some four hundred turnpikes, making it change shape constantly. But what appeared like a series of random unexplained links between passages, had an underlying purpose. Like a Rubik's Cube, a series of algorithms could be used to achieve the desired goal of matching up the colors on the puzzle no matter their position on the cube. In this case, the pieces of the maze kept rotating, but following a well-worn process, they would eventually beat each layer of the maze until they reached the center.

The maze was made up of nine layers, each one consisting of vertical and horizontal passages. Once inside it was hard to tell how much farther one had to go until they reached the next turnpike. The obsidian walls all looked the same.

To make matters worse, the echo of angry predators was a constant, no matter where they were, making it impossible to tell how close they were to the predatory threats.

They entered the maze.

Sam and Tom moved quickly, trying to cover as much ground before the ancient guards reached them. They made it all the way through to the seventh layer before they were greeted with the pride of marsupial lions.

Sam waited until they came near, lifted the barrel of the shotgun and fired once. The lions shied away, having learned last time the meaning of such a sound.

Sam and Tom kept going, keeping close to each other to ensure that none of the lions, finding an opportunity, decided to make their attack.

Again, a single lion came in close and Sam was forced to make another warning shot.

This time, the lion, suspecting a ruse, decided against retreating, and instead pounced forward. Tom reacted first. He didn't fire another warning shot. Those were over now. He aimed for the lion's body and fired twice.

The heavy stopping round killed the animal instantly.

It wasn't something to be proud of, but they didn't have much of a choice. With the apex predator dead, the other lions appeared to lose interest.

Sam and Tom kept moving.

They worked their way through each separate layer of the maze until they reached the final internal walls. These were different from the rest of the maze, which looked like identical, smooth, and glassy obsidian. Instead, this one had multiple petroglyphs etched into the obsidian. There were images of pyramids, sarcophagi, looking glass pedestals, labyrinths, and star constellations. There was a wealth of information there, but he didn't dare give any of them more than a passing glance.

Sam's eyes darted to the wall.

On it was a petroglyph of a maze stretching from the floor up to roughly five feet.

Sam recognized it from their last time.

There were a series of turnpikes hidden in the maze in the form of a raised stone. Sam searched for and depressed each one of them.

The ancient mechanisms behind the wall began to turn.

A few seconds later, they slipped through the ancient wall, leaving the deadly maze, and entering the pristine grounds of the Caretaker's lands at the center of the maze.

Sam's eyes lit up at their new environment.

The center of the maze was covered in verdant grass, with cattle and sheep casually dotted around, grazing peacefully. A massive colonial-style sandstone building stood proudly to the east, overlooking the estate. It reminded him of a castle overlooking its English countryside.

Beside the building stood a smaller one, possibly a set of stables, and a barn for farm animals. A single stream ran from the north to the south of the land, with a single waterwheel feeding its agriculture, and a large opaline lake adorning the center of the paradise.

They kept a rapid steady pace to the colonial estate, entered it, and made their descent into the basement.

Inside, a giant obsidian door was fully open.

There was a message scribbled above its archway.

The ancient journey to Shangri-La is reserved for the bravest of them all...

Sam and Tom glanced at it, excitement in their eyes.

Then they both stepped forward.

Chapter Fifty

Shangri-La

Elise worked furiously to prepare for the attack that was now imminent.

It was nice to finally meet her parents, John and Jenny. They seemed like nice people, although somehow distant. Having grown up thinking she was an orphan, she'd missed that side of her parents.

Her mother had assured her that at one stage, all four of them had lived in Shangri-La, where time passed slowly. They were one big happy family, before internal fighting among the guests, along with a raging debate about the use of the Phoenix Plague, meant that their parents decided it would be safer to separate the kids and send them away.

Besides, it seemed unfair to keep the children in Shangri-La, a place where time was almost entirely stagnant, before they became older.

Elise still couldn't wrap her head around what it all meant.

Apparently, Shangri-La was a sanctuary for all Master Builders. A place where the best of them could come and debate the direction of the human race. The lamasery was usually maintained by a single caretaker, who was ordained with the solemn power to adjudicate between each of the leading Master Builders.

It was a way to balance power.

But it was more than that.

The caretaker, along with his or her panel of eight Master Builders – one from each of the continents – would decide how to wield their immense power for the good of the world. Shangri-La, as well as being a sanctuary, also housed the greatest archives of information about powerful people. The place was a type of fulcrum, capable of leveraging the most benign politician, banker, bureaucrat, diplomat, or CEO.

After the relative peace of the last three thousand years, Shangri-La, having failed to accept new coming Master Builders, had dwindled in its power. Finally, it had succumbed to the loss of its most recent caretaker.

This had resulted in a race to rediscover Shangri-La and seize that power.

And now they waited for their enemies to come.

Chapter-Fifty-One

The man with the blond hair walked through the maze undisturbed by its predator guardians, as he knew they would recognize and fear him. The lions looked at him. The man stared back until they whined and moved away. Like some ancient evil, they instinctively knew when something was wrong.

The blond-haired man entered the center of the maze and walked right up to the caretaker, meeting the man's eye. "Hello."

The caretaker looked at him like he had seen a ghost. "What the hell are you doing back here?"

He held the caretaker's gaze. "You mean, how did I get back after you betrayed me?"

The caretaker didn't buy into the recriminations. "What are you doing here, *Death*?"

"Relax. I'm not here for the 8th Continent. To be honest it was too much work being one of the Ancient Ones, anyway…"

The caretaker's eyes narrowed. His eyes flashed mistrust. "So, then, what do you want?"

"I'm looking for someone… a guy with too much confidence for his own good… and his friend, a veritable giant. Tends to hang out with the first one. Sound familiar?"

The caretaker shook his head. "Afraid not."

Death watched the caretaker's eyes. He was a good liar, but his eyes betrayed him when they darted toward the open obsidian doorway. The ancient door was open. He grinned. "Holy shit… they flicked all the levers… and opened that damned door. It's true then, they're going after Shangri-La."

"I'm afraid so…" The caretaker looked at him. "There's something else you should know."

"What?"

"Someone else made the journey before either of you."

Death pondered that, curiously for a moment. "Who?"

"The one you call Wizard."

He released a big boisterous laugh. "Well, well… it really is one big happy reunion, isn't it?"

Death withdrew an obsidian blade from its sheath, then stabbed the caretaker upward and into his chest. The ancient blade severed the large blood vessel at the bottom of the aorta, killing him within seconds.

"Thanks for the help," he said, and walked through the ancient doorway…

Chapter Fifty-Two

Sam and Tom continued down the pathway.

It seemed to go deeper and deeper underground, which struck Sam as strange, given that they were already five hundred feet below the sea just by being in the 8th Continent. The temperature seemed to warm up as they descended, and soon it became outright hot. Steam rose from the depths far below.

Nearly an hour later, the downward passageway finally leveled out. They continued along a horizontal tunnel for some time.

At the end of it, Sam spotted the cause of the heat.

They were travelling through an active volcano.

The passageway ended at a river of hot, molten lava. It was flowing slowly down a separate tunnel. Sam and Tom exchanged meaningful glances.

Tom's look said – Where in the hell have you brought me?

Sam's look said – We are in the bowels of hell. What the world were we thinking?

Tied up along the shore of the river of lava, were two rafts. Each one made of stone. The stone was dark like obsidian, but coated in something that glistened. Sam couldn't imagine what protected them from melting, but whatever it was, it seemed to be doing a good job of it.

Along the shore was a single wooden placard.

It read, *Shangri-La*.

And was shaped like an arrow pointing downriver.

Sam glanced at the subterranean passage through which lava lazily flowed. His eyes darting between the obsidian raft and Tom. Sam met his eyes. "All right, all aboard!"

Tom said, "You've got to be kidding me!"

"Hey it's been here for thousands of years, why should it sink now?"

"Who knows? But last time I checked hot, molten lava was kind of hot. It's one of those simple truisms of life. Don't go walking in dangerous neighborhoods on your own late at night, don't fly on cheap airlines run by third world nations that are engaged in civil war, oh… and don't go riding in rafts down rivers of lava!"

Sam waited until he was finished. He grinned. "Are you done now?"

"Yeah."

"Feel better?"

"Much. Thank you."

Sam patted him on the shoulder. "Great. Now get on board."

Tom stepped up onto the raft.

Sam untied the rope and pushed off the wall. The raft began floating down the ancient lava river. The river meandered along at a leisurely pace and the raft seemed to travel nicely. Well, there was an exception. At one point, the raft slammed into a wall a little hard, and a small slash of lava splashed onto its deck, narrowly missing their legs.

After about twenty minutes, Sam said to Tom, "What do you think?"

"I don't know." He shook his head. "It kinda puts a whole new spin on Disneyland's Pirates of the Caribbean ride."

Sam held onto the middle of the raft, keeping his balance. "Yeah, I agree. That ride's never going to be quite the same after this."

A little while later, the ceiling of the passageway appeared to be getting shorter. Soon they had to duck just to keep from scraping their heads along the roof. The lava river seemed to be picking up its pace, too. It was as if the river was approaching a waterfall – or in this case, a lavafall.

In the distance, Sam spotted the exact point where the flowing river of molten rock disappeared further underground.

"Oh shit!" they both said in unison.

The raft plowed down toward empty space. Instead of falling however, it became lodged into the rock, remaining afloat, while the hot magma rolled lazily by, before descending into the dark void below.

Tom looked at Sam. "Tell me the map that Jordan gave you mentions this?"

Palms held out, Sam gave a placating gesture. "He didn't mention it."

"Right, well… we'd better work this out, or you're going to be the one I throw overboard to swim back."

Sam stared at the wall to their left.

There were a series of ancient texts, written in the original script of the Master Builders. Next to one of them, Sam spotted a round indentation.

It was the same size of the medallion he wore around his neck.

He withdrew it and placed the medallion into the hold.

After a few seconds, the bronze turned a bright red and golden color, typical of orichalcum – and the gateway gaped open.

Sam and Tom stepped inside.

They shined the beam of a flashlight into the darkness. It wasn't much. More like a small obsidian chamber, barely big enough for the two of them to sit down.

Tom frowned. "Now what?"

Sam shook his head. "I don't know. Jordan didn't mention anything about a cave."

The door shut behind them.

Sam and Tom tried to open it. But the damned thing had sealed them in completely. They ran their hands around the walls, but the entire thing was blocked.

Tom said, "We're trapped!"

Sam licked his lips. "I noticed that too."

A few seconds later, their entire world turned into an empty void. Sam felt as though he was free falling…

Chapter Fifty-Three

The mysterious cave opened into the outside world.

Gone was the darkness. In its place, was the sunny, tropical paradise of Shangri-La. Sam took in the near mythical sanctuary at a glance. The giant vertical walls of hanging gardens looked just like the description of the Hanging Gardens of Babylon or something out of the biblical Garden of Eden, with an array of tropical plants growing out of a giant vertical wall that stretched hundreds of feet high in every direction, hanging miraculously from the sky like a giant, tropical shroud.

Sam squinted against the bright sky through which a warm sunlight poured down upon him. There was something unusual about the beam of sunlight. His eyes narrowed and he tried to work out what it was, but he couldn't put his finger on it. If he had to guess, it just seemed like something was slightly off. As though the light was being dispersed by something opaque.

His eyes drifted to the left, as he slowly turned around, taking in the entire enclave. At the center was a small, almost medieval hamlet consisting of no more than a dozen or so stone houses. These were interspaced with a single large building at the center of which, was a large, natural oasis with crystal clear water, surrounded by sand.

The entire place smelled of the strong scents of exotic fruits which grew freely along the hanging gardens. On a deck of cedar, they spotted two people wearing Hawaiian shirts. An older man and woman. Behind them, Sam met the familiar face of Elise, and walked their way.

She beamed with pleasure at the sight of them.

"Sam!" Her eyes darted toward Tom. "Tom! You found it! I'd like you to meet my parents, John and Jenny."

"Pleased to meet you both," Sam said, dutifully, shaking each of their hands.

"Likewise," Tom said.

"It's nice to meet you," John said. "Elise and Ben have told us so much about you. I'm interested to hear your take on the recent changes in Shangri-La."

Sam said, "I don't really know that much about Shangri-La, except that there has been a recent shift in power, and there's a race to cease it before a new caretaker can become established."

John said, "That just about sums it up. I hope you gentlemen have come prepared to fight."

Sam said, "I thought fighting was forbidden in Shangri-La?"

"That's normally the case, but the rules tend to not apply so much when the caretaker dies."

"So, how do they pick a new caretaker?"

"They already have." John threw him a concerned look. "The old one ordains a new one before his or her death."

"Right. So who's the new caretaker?"

"It's me."

"Okay, so with you in the big chair as the new caretaker, don't the rules apply once more – its forbidden to fight in Shangri-La?"

"I'm afraid that's not how power is established."

Sam suppressed a grin. "Let me get this right, after all these years, the Master Builders are still squabbling over who gets to hold the power?"

"Something like that. Although I'm afraid it's a little more complicated than that when we're talking about this sacred place."

"Why?"

"Shangri-La holds a sort of fulcrum to the world. It has developed a series of archives for the most powerful people on the planet. We, the puppet masters can pull the strings to maintain governments, companies, and ruling parties to ways and means that we believe will keep the human race alive. Increasing in its ability to survive and prosper."

"Yet there are other factions that believe the various parties of the world need to be manipulated to other purposes."

Sam said, "They don't believe the human race should survive?"

John nodded. "Exactly."

"What will happen?"

"When the others arrive?"

"Yeah."

"There will be a fight to the death. We've tried to prepare Shangri-La as best we could, but our numbers are short, and it might be our time to lose control. Although I warn you, if we do, it will have dire consequence for humanity."

Sam could imagine. He gripped his shotgun. "Well, we're prepared to help fight."

John and Jenny Gellie shook their heads. Together, they said, "I'm afraid traditional weapons won't work in here."

"Why not?"

"There's a magnetic field surrounding Shangri-La."

Sam held the shotgun. "It looks balanced to me."

"Try shooting it."

Sam squeezed the trigger. The shot seemed to misfire. He squeezed the trigger again and found the same response. A puzzled expression crept over Sam's face. "What's happening?"

"It has to do with the velocity. The magnetic field affects high velocity metal projectiles."

"I have a knife."

"It won't help. We all have our own weapons."

"We?" Sam asked.

John said, "Oh, yes. We're not entirely on our own."

Chapter Fifty-Four

Sam looked at the strange man from the Winter Temple. He wore the erudite expression of an ancient, and learned being. Up close, Sam could see that the staff he carried actually had an orb at the end of it. It reminded Sam of the Ark of Light he'd found in the Mahogany Ship.

John said, "Ah, I see you've already met Wizard."

Sam greeted the man. "Wizard?"

"I'm four hundred years old and reader of a great many things. As it would seem, people find it difficult to differentiate between wizards and those who are learned. Either way, I was given the name, and now it's stuck."

Sam threw him a I can't see how they would pick that sort of name for you type of expression.

Ben Gellie turned up, carrying two crossbows. He handed them to Tom and Sam.

Sam made a wry smile. "Master Builders have ruled the planet for thousands upon thousands of years, built some of the greatest temples on earth, and you're going to fight out the ultimate battle of good versus evil using medieval weapons?"

Ben shrugged. "The crossbow's made of wood. The bolts are wood. Not metal components. When the battle rages, it will be the most lethal thing in Shangri-La."

Wizard arched his eyebrows, but he remained silent.

Ben said, "Except for you, Wizard. Everyone knows a wizard is the most dangerous thing in a battlefield."

Wizard let out a satisfactory sigh.

Sam and Tom checked their crossbows. Grabbed a quiver full of bolts and tried out a few shots. The weapons were surprisingly easy to use and accurate. Elise turned up a few minutes later, carrying a longbow. John and Jenny arrived, armed with obsidian spears.

Sam ran his eyes across the strange array of medieval weapons and their ragamuffin band of unlikely warriors.

Sam asked, "Now what do we do?"

John replied, "Now, we wait for them to come."

Chapter Fifty-Five

Two hours later, a loud explosion indicated that they had arrived.

Giant cracks began to form across the opaque blue sky. Whatever dome had concealed and protected Shangri-La throughout the eons, was in the process of being permanently destroyed. Tons of ice fell from it, devastating the tropical hanging gardens. Their entire world was about to be ripped apart.

John's face twisted into a mask of incognizant fury. Tears sheeted down his cheeks, but no sound came with them. After a good thirty seconds, he breathed out. "I don't believe it."

"Believe what?" Sam asked.

"They've broken through the physical location. They haven't made the journey to Shangri-La via the traditional gateways."

Sam asked, "How does that change anything?"

"It changes everything." John was horrified. "Don't you see, they're no longer restricted to one or two Master Builders per gateway. Instead, they're going to assault Shangri-La with massive numbers of soldiers."

Sam said, "No one has ever known the physical location of Shangri-La?"

"That's right! Not since the original Master Builders constructed it. That's what makes it so special. Only the brightest, most noble, are able to survive the journey just to reach it. It makes it the perfect gateway to exclusion."

Sam felt like this was starting to sound more and more like an ego driven cult, than an ancient race, hell bent on saving the human race. "No one's ever reached its physical location without the gateways? Not ever?"

John said, "There was one guy… his plane crashed. It landed in some mountain range, somewhere, and while he was trying to find his way home, he fell, landing in Shangri-La."

Sam smiled. "Let me guess, his name was James Hilton and he became a novelist."

"How did you know?"

"Easy guess." Sam curbed the ghost of a smile. "He wrote a book about it."

"I know. We let him do it. In fact, we helped him write it. The thing might not have been such a success without us."

"Why?"

"Our numbers were dwindling. We needed to find a way to reach other descendants of Master Builders."

"So, you mean something in the book works like a cipher, triggering a response in people with the right DNA?"

"Right again. Hey, you're good at this."

"Thanks. But what are we going to do now that Shangri-La's physical location has been found?" Sam asked, his voice hard as steel. "Is there anything we can do?"

Johns reply was emphatic. "No. All is lost."

"Not everything." Jenny replied. "There's still time to destroy Shangri-La and protect its secrets."

Sam asked, "How?"

"There's a built in safety system designed to protect the secret knowledge in the case that Shangri-La is ever overrun."

"How does it work?"

"This whole region is built into a semi-active volcano. There's dynamite rigged up to an old lava tube. If we blow it, a volcanic river will flood Shangri-La – effectively wiping the entire slate clean and burying her secrets forever."

Elise said, "Do you want me to come with you?"

"No," her mother said, giving her a long hug. "I'm afraid this is a one-way journey."

"What do you mean?" Elise cried out, revealing a level of emotions that Sam had never seen before. "I've only just got my family back, and now you're leaving me again!"

Her dad held her. "I'm so sorry. We weren't the best parents, but we tried our best to do what we thought was right for you."

"What was right was to stay together. That's always what's right for a family! That's all I ever wanted!"

"I know… it's what we wanted too." Her mother said, "But there were things – bigger things than our own happiness – which needed us. I'm sorry. But I'm so glad that we got the chance to spend this week together, and that you will always have your brother."

There was so much Elise wanted to say, but there wasn't time. And she was worried if she said anything else, it would come out as a series of unforgivable recriminations, which would haunt her for the rest of her life.

Instead she simply hugged both of her parents goodbye, and said, "I love you both so much."

John said, "Try to hold them off as long as you can until we get into the catacombs. Then, you must all make your way to the gateways and leave Shangri-La."

Sam said, "Good luck."

Chapter Fifty-Six

Minutes later, elite soldiers began to rappel down from the fractured sky.

The preliminary group of twenty or so soldiers landed on the opposite end of the hanging gardens and began setting up a perimeter from which to regroup.

Sam, Tom, and Ben waited with the crossbows. The medieval weapons would never fire so far. Elise, with her English longbow, began to pick off targets as they abseiled, but Wizard cautioned her to wait. She didn't have enough arrows in her quiver to take half of them.

More than a hundred mercenaries flooded into their attacker's makeshift fortress. They were carrying spears and daggers of fractured obsidian. The whole thing looked surreal and medieval. Slowly, their attackers prepared to make their assault.

Wizard stood up and stuck his staff into the ground. The sunlight filled the orb, magnifying it, until the pressure, became too great for the orb to withhold.

A beam of sunlight erupted from his staff, striking the emboldened group of attackers, like a giant explosion.

Screams of agony filled the once peaceful world of Shangri-La.

As the rubble settled, those attackers who survived, began to run at them – their weapons in hand.

Sam, Tom, and Ben began to release crossbow bolts, making well-placed shots into the torsos of their enemies. Elise drew an arrow, shooting them in quick succession. Wizard fired another burst of sunrays. The beam hit the hanging garden, turning it into a vertical forest fire, and burning the third wave of soldiers who had begun to rappel down from the sky.

Wizard turned to the rest of them. "We must leave."

Elise looked pained, as though she wanted to cry out that there was still time for her parents to make it. But the logical, reasonable, part of her knew that it wasn't true. She fired another arrow, and then turned to leave.

Coming face to face with *Death*.

Wizard smirked. "You're too late, *Death*."

Death ran his eyes across the bloodied battlefield. "What are you talking about? It looks like I've arrived just in time."

Wizard said, "You won't win."

"That's for me to decide."

"No. I mean, you can't have Shangri-La."

"I've always been more powerful than you, brother. I'll take it."

"No. You're missing the point. John and Jenny have already begun the process of destroying Shangri-La to protect her secrets!"

"They can't!" *Death* looked frightened for the first time in more than a century. "They can't destroy everything that Shangri-La has to offer! Think of the loss!"

Wizard laughed. "You still don't get it, do you? Some people don't crave power."

"Everyone craves power!" *Death* stepped up close to Wizard and drove his obsidian knife into the man's guts.

Wizard gave a sardonic laugh, full of fury and mirth. "It's over... for all of us."

"Not for me it isn't brother!" *Death* began to make a run for the catacombs.

Elise drew another arrow, aimed, and released it.

The shot flew straight and true, piercing right through *Death's* chest. The ancient Master Builder turned to meet her eyes. His face twisted with a mixture of disbelief, loss, and then finally as he expired, peace.

Sam, Tom, Ben, and Elise didn't wait to see how the rest of the battle played out. They climbed into the waiting obsidian cave.

Sam said, "Are you ready?"

Elise said, "Give them just a little while longer."

"I don't know if we have much longer..."

A few seconds later, the explosion ripped through the mountain high above them. The subsequent avalanche was instantaneous. Large boulders of rock and ice began to fall, pelting down on the once utopic village of Shangri-La.

Lava began to flow from beneath the catacombs, rising up like a tsunami, killing everyone in its path before it engulfed what remained of Shangri-La.

Sam said, "That's enough!"

He placed the medallion onto its keypad, spun the medallion three clicks to the right and stepped inside.

Elise had tears in her eyes. "It's not fair. I only just got to meet my parents, and now they're gone! They gave their lives for us."

Ben said, "Not just us. They gave their lives for humanity."

Sam turned to Elise. It was the first time he'd seen her show any sign of her emotions. "Are you going to be okay?"

She closed her eyes, took a deep breath, and opened them again. She met his gaze directly. "Yeah, it's going to be okay. I know that they had a good life. It lasted more than three hundred years – a lot more than anyone's entitled to – I just wish I'd gotten to spend more than the last week getting to know them."

Sam squeezed her hand. "I understand."

A moment later, the dark void in the cave disappeared.

And they were taken away from the legendary paradise, leaving Shangri-La forever...

Chapter Fifty-Seven

Strait of Gibraltar – One Week Later...

On board the *Tahila* Matthew greeted Sam Reilly, bringing him up to speed about the general running of the ship.

Catarina stepped out of Sam's quarters. Her hair was still wet, like she'd just stepped out of the shower. She met Sam with a radiant smile, before kissing him affectionately. She pulled him in tight and squeezed his waist.

Sam withdrew, trying to conceal his grimace. He squeezed her hands. "It's good to see you. When did you get in?"

"About an hour ago."

Sam recalled that she had just presented her thesis on memory databases to some of the world leaders in neurology. "How was your conference in Venice?"

"Good. It went really well." Her eyes ran across his body with the scrutiny of a trained surgeon, landing on his face. His jaw was taut, his lips held tight, as though suppressing something. She smiled, either not registering his discomfort, or pretending to ignore it. "How have you been?"

"Good," Sam replied, his voice non-committal.

"Matthew tells me you found Shangri-La," she said, casually.

"Yeah, but it's been destroyed."

"That's a shame. Matthew told me that, too. Apparently, it was built high in the Himalayas?"

Sam nodded. "Yeah, satellite images recorded a large section at the eastern side of Everest collapse. There was no sign of Shangri-La, but analysis of the avalanche matches up with an explosion with a subsequent collapse of mountain at the identical time that Shangri-La was destroyed."

"Did Elise find what she was looking for?"

"Yes and no. She found her parents, but lost them again week later, when they sacrificed their lives to protect us."

"I'm sorry." Catarina's voice genuine and full of empathy. "Is Elise all right?"

"I think so. She's grateful to have got the chance to meet them, even if it was for such a short duration."

"And you're okay?"

"Yeah. I'm okay."

"That's good." Her eyes leveled on his. "So, are you going to tell me what new injuries you have?"

"Nothing much..." Sam's eyes drifted toward the floor. His voice sheepish. "I had an incident a few weeks ago. I'm still a bit tender from the surgery, that's all."

She was grinning now. "You had surgery? What surgery did you have, Sam?"

Sam was squirming now. "I don't know the name of it. You know me, I'm not really the medical type of guy. I'm happy to leave that up to the professionals."

Catarina turned to Matthew, whose lips were curled in a wide grin, beaming at Sam's discomfort. "Hey Matthew, you want to tell me what surgery my boyfriend had a few ago?"

Matthew began to laugh. Addressing Sam, incredulity plastered across his face, he said, "You didn't mention to Catarina that you got shot?"

Sam turned his palms skyward. He looked at Catarina. "I was going to get around to it. In my defense, I've been pretty busy since I came around after surgery."

Catarina shook her head. "Oh, Sam... you got shot again?"

"Afraid so."

"For someone who's generally good at so many things, you can be really careless at times." Her voice was stern, her tone mocking. "I'm glad you didn't get yourself killed."

Sam said, "Me too."

Caliburn gave a curt bark.

Catarina exhaled a breath. "Sam, is there something else you want to tell me?"

He swallowed. "I don't think so."

"Matthew?" she asked, "Can you think of anything else I might want to know about Sam?"

Matthew, making no effort to conceal his obvious pleasure, said, "He also crashed a helicopter?"

"Really?" she asked.

Sam nodded. "Afraid so."

She pulled him in gently, and kissed his forehead. "You really are a child at times, aren't you?"

"Yeah… so I've been told."

Matthew frowned. "Wait, you're letting him off?"

Catarina shrugged. "Hey, Sam can't help the way he is. It's not his fault he can be stupid at times."

"Ridiculously stupid," Sam agreed, happy that she was letting him off for neglecting to mention that he'd been shot a few weeks ago and needed life-saving surgery.

Matthew stopped laughing. He said, "Oh, by the way, you've got a letter."

"I'll check my emails tonight," Sam said, before pausing. He shot Matthew a smile. "How did you know I have an email?"

"I don't know anything about any emails," Matthew said with a chuckle. "I'm talking about a real letter."

"Wait, the *Tahila's* forty miles off the coast of Spain, how the hell did you receive a letter?"

"By helicopter actually."

Sam was incredulous. "What sort of person hand delivers a letter to a ship out in the middle of the ocean by helicopter?"

Matthew returned fire with a knowing smile. "Someone very intent on ensuring the recipient actually receives the said letter, I suppose."

Sam could only imagine the sort of person who would make such a grandiose gesture. It was the sort of wasteful extravagant act that even his father, as rich as he was, would frown upon.

"All right," Sam said, a rueful smile creasing his lips. "Where's the letter?"

"I left if for you on the round table."

Sam picked up the envelope. "Thanks, Matthew. Did he or she leave a message for me?"

Matthew smirked. "It's a she and I believe you'll find any message she's left for you would traditionally be in the letter."

"Very good, Matthew." Sam refused to bite.

He ran his eyes across the letter...

It was a short, succinct missive. Written in a neat scrawl.

Mr. Sam Reilly,

You are hereby requested to give a talk about maritime archeology, and your experience locating the Mahogany Ship, to a select group of residents on board the prestigious cruise ship known as The World.

At the end of the letter, there was a note.

Afterward, I would like to talk to you about something I believe you might be interested in. I am in possession of some knowledge that I believe might reveal the location of Alexander the Great's ancient treasure.

It was then signed,

Airlie Chapman

Intrigued, Sam smiled, his eyes sparkling with interest.

Tom entered the room and said, "What are you smirking about?"

"I'm not smirking. I was just thinking it's time we go on a proper vacation."

"Okay, where do you want to go?"

Sam grinned. "We're going on a cruise on board *The World*, to be exact. It's one of those ritzy cruise ships that caters for the ultra-rich. Someone has requested I give a talk about our discovery of the *Mahogany Ship* there. Afterward our esteemed guests would like a meet and greet."

"Sure, why not. I can be convinced."

"Good, because after that, someone there wants to talk to us about going on a treasure hunt." Sam turned his attention to Catarina. "Do you want to join us?"

She shook her head. "I'm sorry. I can't play adventurer with you this week, I have to get back to work."

"Okay," Sam said, turning to Tom. "It's just you and me."

"Ah," Tom said, throwing him a look as though it was all making more sense now. "What are we looking for?"

Sam grinned. "The lost treasure of Alexander the Great."

The End

Printed in Great Britain
by Amazon

23839496R00128